Quit Bugging Me

By
Karen Laven

An Aspirations Media Publication

An Aspirations Media™ Publication
www.aspirationsmediainc.com

Copyright © 2007 by Karen Laven
Cover by Tiffany Prothero
Layout by Jennifer Rowell
Design: Jennifer Rowell and Karen Laven

LIBRARY OF CONGRESS CONTROL NUMBER: 2007928475

IBSN: 978-0-9776043-6-4

MANUFACTURED IN THE UNITED STATES

First Printing July 2007

Thanks to Amy Laven, my sister-in-law and dear friend, for sending me "the link" that ultimately gave <u>Quit Bugging Me</u> a home.

Thanks to Sherry Strub for her literary expertise and endless unselfishness in sharing it.

My immense gratitude also goes to Kristine Julig Farkas: an avid reader, intelligent muse and all-around hilariously funny broad. Thanks, Kris, for reading, rereading, rereading and (just once more...please?) rereading your little sis' debut YA novel. I know, at times, it felt like the bugs were coming out of your ears! Be assured that the honest, forthright input from you translated into a deeper, richer output from me.

Additionally, thanks to those family, friends and teachers who nudged me forward along this oft-rocky writers path with their faith, support, empathy and wit. (It mattered greatly to me 20 years ago, and it matters now.)

Thanks to the most important "men" in my life (you know, you three guys lounging around in the living room). Oh, and Luke? You are right; I couldn't have done it without you.

I also thank you, the reader, for taking the time to see what this wacky "bug book" is really all about. I sure hope you enjoy reading it as much as I enjoyed writing it.

Finally, thanks to Lee and everybody at Aspirations Media, for giving <u>Quit Bugging Me</u> life and for making the evolution process so much fun.

Karen

For Doug, Jake and Luke...
I pray that we will be blessed with many more years together,
"bugging" each other...You have given me the best times of my life.

chapter
One

Date: March 23, 2005 **Time:** 7:42 p.m. CST
To: MRobbins@mned.comp
From: Elockhardt@wryword.comp
Subject: *HELP! To my gorgeous eighth-grade teacher! From her adoring student, Emily Lockhardt*

Dear, dear, Mrs. Robbins...I can't do my spring report on bugs! I can't! I've tried, and I can't! I hate bugs. Truly. Yesterday, my brother (who was unbelievably excited that I'd have to do a paper on insects) brought me a book he'd just received. Anyway, the book's called "Bugs: Up Close and Real Personal." What are the odds? *(Pretty great, if it's about torturing me.)*

It has the most realistic photographs of those hideous things that I have ever seen—including a picture of this gigantic millipede on the cover. I gave it back and told him I wouldn't be needing it after all, because I was sure you were going to answer my plea and let me switch my topic. Anyway, when I went downstairs to answer the phone—it was just Angelina, bragging about her new shoes again—that must have been when Bud (that's my brother—you had him two years ago...remember?) stuck that horrible bug book of his under my pillows (I always sleep with three).

Mrs. Robbins, last night I had the most horrible nightmare about those millipedes! They were living in my pillow—thousands of them. My head was smack dab in the middle of their squirming multi-legged bodies, as they slithered over my forehead, up my nose, inside my ears, boring through—trying to reach my brain! Some of them even forced their way under my eyelids. The pain was unbearable! I'll never forget the feeling of all those legs over my face and their feet (?) scratching my corneas. When Mom came in and woke me up, I was gagging on something and honestly, Mrs. Robbins, it felt like a millipede. I know you'll say that's impossible, but I swear, when I tried to cough it up, I…I felt it scurry down my throat. I told Mom and she laughed and said Stephen King should watch his back. She thinks the "millipede" was just mucus. But Mrs. Robbins, since when does mucus skitter?

This morning I checked my pillows for holes and stuff, (that's how real my dream was), and when I lifted them up, that gargantuan millipede on the cover of Bud's bug book was staring RIGHT at me. And I swear, it was grinning. I ran out of my room, through the kitchen (right past Bud, who was inhaling his waffles) and threw his horrible bug book down the cellar stairs. Needless to say, I'm not speaking to him ever again—for a very long time.

Mrs. Robbins—please! Don't make me do my report on bugs! Please! Look what they've already put me through! They are the ugliest, lowliest creatures on this earth, and I hate them. They're creepy and crawly, sluggy and slimy. Some scamper under your bed, while others are busy munching on your skin while you're in bed, watching the spider on the ceiling dangle overhead. Still other varieties slither beneath a pile of dirty, damp clothes.

And did you know that they grow inside your favorite cereal? They can even sometimes be found wriggling in the flour that mom's making chocolate cake with. There are even bugs that live on your HEAD. Lice. I know of their ways first hand—they called my long blonde hair home just last winter. UGH! My mom sat huddled above me with a magnifying glass and flashlight for HOURS—ripping their eggs off of my scalp, endlessly pursuing the long, black live ones. It was like a scene straight out of the jungle. Not to mention the scratching. My family walked around continuously for two weeks with our hands on our heads.

And you want me to do my report on bugs? Mrs. Robbins...do you dislike me that much? Am I so des...um, pickable?

Hey, I just got an idea! Why not have Lyle Lahrvey do it? He LOVES bugs! Loves them! Why, just last week he boasted that he had tried to revive a squashed beetle by performing chest compressions. Oh, please, tell me Lyle and I can switch assignments. He'll do my report on bugs and I'll do his report on the prairie. Why, if I'd been alive a century ago, Laura Ingalls Wilder and I would have been best friends—for sure. That Nellie would have been running for the hills.

Oh, please, please, PLEASE let us switch. Please! You're my favorite teacher, you know. Truly. I've never told you before because I didn't want that to influence my grades. Not that you would EVER let that happen. Oh please, e-mail me back soon with your reply. Mom says I can stay up until midnight tonight, if necessary. She says you might be on a "date" with Mr. Robbins—dancing or something. Well, I guess that's sort of possible—I mean you do look so young!!! Mom'll let me wait up because SHE knows how important this is to me. Please remember and never forget...you're my favorite teacher, you're gorgeous, oh-so-youthful looking and remarkably stunning, and I HATE BUGS!!!!!! Most Sincerely, Emily Lockhardt

• •

Date: March 23, 2005 **Time:** 10:01 CST
From: MRobbins@mned.comp
From: Elockhardt@wryword.comp
Subject: *Re: HELP! To my gorgeous eighth-grade teacher! From her adoring student, Emily Lockhardt*

Dear Emily, my sycophant student, such a literate and vibrant imagination you have! I do not dislike—nor have I ever disliked—you. You are certainly not "despicable," by any means. I was very pleased to hear from you. I am glad you are utilizing your computer and my e-mail address. Knowledge is a powerful tool and it shall take you far. Oh, yes, I do remember your brother, Bud. Very well, in fact. The poor dear...tell me, has his face cleared up?

Now, down to the nitty gritty. You made a powerful case, concerning your abhorrence for bugs, and I must admit I was compelled to check my flour and my son, Leonard's, Kaptain Munch Cereal for tiny "critters" as soon as I'd finished your message. Quite honestly, the content of your e-mail made my skin crawl.

Isn't that wonderful? That's exactly the sort of passion and punch your upcoming report needs. I am sure it will be a real winner.

In spite of (or perhaps because of) your well-versed plea, I have decided that you shall do the report on bugs, and Lyle Lahrvey will report on the prairie. Why? Because you both can chart new territory, cover new ground—and learn something new!

Lyle has agreed to keep an open mind concerning his report, and I must also remind you that one does not need to be a fan of "Little House on the Prairie" books to pen a report about the aforementioned ecosystem.

Now, Emily dear, please don't let this dishearten you. This is for your own good...trust me. Please always remember—especially when you feel "bugged down," (so to speak), that "thankflea," (ha) your academic year under my supervision will soon bee; (a little bit of bug humor!) but a memory. Have an enjoyable weekend, and I'll see you bright and early Monday!

Sincerely,

Your (once?) favorite teacher, Mrs. Robbins

• •

Date: March 24, 2005 **Time:** 4:56 p.m. CST.
To: JoelJin@surftwn.comp
From: Elockhardt@wryword.comp
Subject: *I hate bugs and Mrs. Robbins!*

Oh Joel. I am about to collapse with disgust! That evil, ancient, decrepit-looking Mrs. Robbins is making me do that icky report on bugs after all. How much does one 13-year-old lady have to bear?

She expects me to actually research things like slugs (UGH!) and earwigs, for crying out loud. Why, if I have to do that I'll puke. (Speaking of puking, Mom's calling me to dinner. Meatloaf's on the menu—not the nummy kind she used to make though. No ketchup, no grease, no taste. Now she only uses ground turkey instead of hamburger. Gross.)

You know, I can tell she doesn't like me…(Mrs. Robbins, not my mom). She's probably jealous of my youth and lack of wrinkles—what do you think?

I've got this wrinkly old, old, OLD teacher on my case and then Bud puts a disgusting bug book under my pillow and all of the sudden I'm going crazy. How can that be? It's like they're in cahoots with each other. The old bat teacher and my too skinny brother. He is such a dork. A too dopey, too messy, too dirty dishwater blonde-headed, too zit-faced (well, there's a couple of them left at least) dork! I try so hard not to let him bother me but he does. He bothers me more than anybody in this world. Now that I think of it, brother is really bother without the "r." Who ever invented that word had it right, alright. This kid who half the time forgets to put deodorant under BOTH arms, is making ME lose my sanity! That's just ridiculous. If you were here I could get through all this buggy mess, Joel.

Joel, I am so confused and I miss you!!! I wish you hadn't deserted me and gone to California. Minnesota just isn't the same without you. I miss your tallness. It made me look even more petite than I already am. I miss your jet-black crew cut and your goofy smile. I miss you being HERE up north where you're supposed to be.

I bet your teacher is real young and laid back and tan and stuff. I bet she says, Hey dudes, shall we read on the beach today? And I'll bet you all say yeah, man that'd be cool…I bet you slouch now and have let your hair grow out like your zillions of surfer friends. Don't be cool, Joel. Be you!

Why aren't you HERE when I NEED you?

Hey! Maybe I'll run away and stay with you and your family! Wouldn't that be great? The two "EmJo's" together again. Oh, if my life could just be the WAY IT USED TO BE.

Joel, something's happening to me—and it's not good. It's bad. I have to tell you about this dream (?) I had last night. I was literally drowning in millipedes—really! All those millions of legs…it was positively horrifying, but the worst part was…it felt sooooo reeaalll!!! I'm scared.

Uh-oh. Mom's doin' that screechy thing with her voice, yelling that dinner will be ruined. (How could we ever tell?) She can't find Bud. He's probably off in the woods again. Mom says one day those woods might just swallow him up. Really, I don't know what he does out there. If you think about it, a 150-acre nature preserve is an easy place to get lost in. But he always seems to find his way back out, darn it. Anyway, I'd better sign off for now.

But, Joel, honestly, I feel real edgy like the worse is yet to come and I can't shake it. The truth is, I'm not sure it was just a dream…I think it might have really happened…

Em

• •

Date: March 24, 2005 **Time:** 6:04 p.m. CST.
To: Elockhardt@wryword.comp
From: JoelJin@surftwn.comp
Subject: *Re: I hate bugs and Mrs. Robbins!*

Hey Em:

What might have really happened? Drowning in millipedes? What the heck are you talking about Em? You gotta e-mail me back! You can't leave me hanging! Speaking of hanging, some of the kids in the neighborhood have asked me if I wanna go hang 10 with them next week. That means surf. I think.

As for the bug report, Em, it won't take you long to come up with a decent paper—remember you're not only gorgeous—you're brilliant. (I'm quoting from the Christmas card you sent me this year.) Relax! Try and keep it loose, Em. Boy, are you dramatic. You act dramatic and you sure write dramatic. You're the only person I know who actually spell checks their emails.

You know darn well you'll see the entire Jinkins family on April 1st—that's only a week or so away. You'll be happy to know that my hair is still spiked and my legs are still way too long for my body. I tripped over nothing just walking into English yesterday right in front of Melanie Dorn. Man, Melanie Dorn. No cool hanging 10 dude here.

It'll be sweet to get back to Minnesota for a few days over spring break. Ma misses your mom, Pop wants to check out your Dad's new table saw (weird but what's new), and as for Janice (aka Queen of Mean)? Well, she asked if she could stay behind in California alone. Su-weet as su-weet can be! Unfortunately my folks won't let her. Obviously, she hasn't changed much since you last saw her...

Anyway, Em, just go ahead and do the bug report—I promise, it'll be over before ya know it.

Say...did ya save me a big hunk of cold turkey meatloaf? Num num. Ya know it really does sound pretty good. Since coming out here Mom's been making SUPER healthy cruddy stuff like tofu burgers. I don't know what tofu is, but it isn't good and it sure is not meat. Get back to me soon.

Joel

Date: March 25, 2005 **Time:** 10:00 a.m. CST.
To: JoelJin@surftwn.comp
From: Elockhardt@wryword.comp
Subject: *Nightmare that's real!*

I'm sorry I couldn't get back to you sooner, but Dad put his foot down and made us all play cards together last night. It's hard to believe that it was the best part of the evening Joel, but it was. Because what happened afterwards...I can't tell anyone but you. No one else would believe me. Joel, I almost died last night and it's all because of Bud's horrible bug book...

chapter TWo

To: JoelJin@surftwn.comp
From: Elockhardt@wryword.comp *(Continued)*

I don't know where to start. If I don't dare tell you—my best friend in this—or any other—galaxy, then whom can I tell? First, I must ask you to promise that you will erase this e-mail immediately after reading it. I don't want anyone else to see it and think I'm nuts. Especially your sister, Janice… even though she already thinks I'm nuts.

Remember how I told you I "dreamt" my head was covered in millipedes? Joel, it was too real to be only a dream, but still I'd convinced myself that it probably was, because how could it possibly be real? Well, after what happened last night, I think "reality" is something I want no part of. Please, trust me, what follows ISN'T A JOKE! Remember our sacred pinkie swear? Consider it a done deal by me and read on…

Last night we finished playing Crazy 8's about 10:30 and I was ready for bed. (I still haven't talked to Bud, but I sure sneer at him a lot.)

I hadn't slept well the night before (what with millions of millipedes all over my face) so I was pretty anxious to get a "bug-free" night of peaceful sleep.

I was under my covers by a quarter to eleven and had already begun to doze off when I heard it. It was a clicking sound—really kind of soft—at first—but the noise grew and grew until it sounded as loud as rain on a tin roof—really loud, and at first I couldn't tell where it was coming from, but when I heard the sound of my metal hangers banging against the wood, I realized it was coming from the closet.

I slipped out from under my quilt and crept my way towards the noise. It was growing louder with every step I took. I kept waiting for Mom and Dad to rush in to see what the obnoxious sound was. When I got to the double doors of the closet, I reached out and touched the wood. I could feel it vibrating.

Looking back, I don't know why I didn't go get Mom and Dad—or even Bud, or at the very least turn my bedroom light on. What a dope. But for some bizarre reason, I didn't even think of it. I just felt compelled—I MEAN COMPELLED—to open that closet door. Just a crack…just a crack…and peek inside. Slowly, I grasped hold of the knob and pulled the tiniest bit. I couldn't see anything, so I yanked it open wider and that's when I realized that the sound had stopped. I turned on the closet light—and all I saw was red. Everywhere.

Joel, as you well know, I do not look my best in red attire, hence I don't have any red clothes (not counting that yucky Christmas sweater from Aunt Mavis), so, of course I wondered if my eyes were screwing up.

Then I felt a searing pain in my big toe. I reached for it and found it—covered in something…lots of somethings—and they were moving. I stumbled over to my nightlight (I have that for safety reasons only, of course) and stuck my wriggling foot beneath it. It was smothered in bright red ants! You

11

couldn't even tell there was a foot there. I recognized that they were fire ants; I remember that Bud had told me about them once.

Almost immediately, my other bare foot was writhing in pain, and before I could even begin to comprehend what was happening to me, I felt them march up my legs. Literally *march*—like it was some sort of fire drill or something. Row-by-row, they stormed upward.

Frantically, I tried to brush them off, but it didn't work. They latched onto my palms and attacked me there.

Soon they were covering my body—I remember the strange feeling of a bunch of them in the hollow of my neck. Then I felt some of them trickle up my chin. My stomach dropped. I realized then that I was probably going to die. How can an almost 14-year-old woman be killed in her room in late winter by fire ants?

I kept mumbling that "this can't be happening—it can't be happening—I'm dreaming again, wake up...*WAKE UP!*" But I couldn't wake up...because I wasn't asleep. When they reached my mouth, I shut it tight, so they marched up my nostrils. Oh the agony! The room spun and I dropped to the carpet.

How could I possibly still be around to write this to you? Amazingly enough, just about the time I realized I was choking on all those tiny bodies, the door opened and in peeked Mom. Her pink flannel robe was untied and her bangs were sticking up all over the place. She swept them out of her eyes and whispered that she thought she heard a huge thump...She asked me if I was okay and *why* I was sprawled out on the carpet.

The hall light illuminated my body, lying there on the floor—and get this...not one fire ant in sight. They were gone. Completely, totally gone. The pain was immediately gone too.

I had no idea what I was going to say and then in stormed Bud. He was talking about not being able to sleep and needing something to read and then of course *he* had to ask why I was on the floor.

I was so relieved to see both of them—I actually jumped up and hugged Mom, then Bud. He was so shocked that he actually hugged me back for a second. But then he pushed me away and said something like, "Man, you're so weird."

I think I saw Mom nod in agreement before she told me to get back into bed and returned to her room.

Bud crossed to the closet, swung it wide open, (I thought I was going to puke), turned on the light and reached into the far corner. About then I felt like I was going to faint. Soon he pulled out—now you're not going to believe this either—that darn bug book of his.

Bud laughed and told me that after I threw it in the basement, he wasn't going to let me near it again but then he thought, hey! that means she doesn't want it anywhere near her. So, naturally he felt it was his brotherly obligation to hide it in my room. Brothers are warped.

Joel, he stared down at the book and looked confused (I know, I know, Bud looking confused is an oxymoron) but he really did look strange. He stood there tapping the glossy pages and asked why it was open and if I'd actually been reading it.

I jerked my head back and forth and when my eyes fell on the page, I started shaking. There, staring at me from the page was a photo of thousands of fire red, fire ants.

For a split second I swear I saw them wiggling. I ran out of there and into the bathroom. I was so freaked out, I couldn't even squeak, let alone talk. Bud called me a weirdo again, took the book and went into his room.

I wondered if maybe I was going crazy. Almost frantically, I checked my arms and legs…nothing. My face? Looked the same as it always did. Joel, there was absolutely no sign of all the bites I'd just endured. NOTHING!

I couldn't sleep at all after that. I kept wondering if they were going to attack Bud next. I guess they didn't do anything though. The way he sleeps, who can be sure?

Okay, I gotta sign off now, Mom has to call great Aunt Betty. It's like her 120th birthday or something. (Yes, that's the aunt from Minnetonka with the moustache as full as Dad's.) I keep telling mom we need two lines. Joel, I'm afraid to go to bed tonight. You can bet I'm going to search my room from the ceiling down for that darn bug book. Bud would never believe me if I told him what's been happening.

I gotta go, she's screeching again. Erase this NOW, Joel. E-mail me back tomorrow night. Mom and Dad will be at the Lowell's playing poker and Bud's got baseball practice. Boy, I wish you were here—more than I've ever wished anything in my life. What's going to happen tonight? I don't want to know.

Em

chapter Three

Date: March 26, **Time:** 7:03 p.m. CST.
To: Elockhardt@wryword.comp
From: JoelJin@surftwn.comp
Subject: *Re: Nightmare that's real!*

Hey, Em…you're kinda scaring me here. Are you okay? Why haven't you e-mailed me today yet? Man, the suspense is there if that's what you're after. I woulda logged on sooner, but we all went out to eat at a sushi joint. Raw fish, right off the hook, as in hand me a vomit bag. Everybody else loved it. I was actually wishing I had a lame tofu burger. Anyway, Em, if you are there—LET ME KNOW!

I guess you must be eating or something (and I know you aren't eating sushi), but I need to know all's okay. I need to know that last night wasn't full of some creatures slithering all over you. Aw, what's goin' on? This isn't some kind of trick, is it? You write like it's your latest short story or something, Em. If so, it's really good. I already know you're a good writer with a genius vocabulary. I know you're going to be super famous one day (just like you wrote on my birthday card). So, it's okay to tell me it's a story, okay? Cause if it is a story and you're not telling me that would be mean, Em…real mean. Are you still mad at me because my

15

Mom got transferred out to Burbank? Because, IT ISN'T MY FAULT. Don't you know that? So, if this is some sort of game to shake me up? IT'S WORKING! Listen, tell me it's a game, so I can get a good night's sleep. Since you first told me about all this, all I do is lay there (with no pillow) staring at my closet, wondering if you're okay, and when I do actually sleep, I dream of creepy insects partying all over me.

I promise, if you've been making all this up, I'll forgive you. Heck, I'll invest in your career as a screenwriter, if I ever get money. I'm going to sign off and wait for you to e-mail me back. I'll be sitting right here, in front of my laptop. I won't hang 10, I won't hang nothin', I won't budge, unless it's to grab my stash of chockoroo cookies. Man, Mom would kill me if she knew I had three boxes hidden under Q of Means and my bathroom sink.

Joel

• •

Date: March 26, 2005 **Time:** 9:06 p.m. CST.
To: JoelJin@surftwn.comp
From: Elockhardt@wryword.comp
Subject: *Re: Nightmare that's real!*

Joel, I can't believe you'd think I was making all this up. I'm so hurt. But thanks for the kudos about my writing skills. Screenwriting has always been a dream of mine. I would like to not only write, but also star in my own productions. Anyway, darn it! You are the ONLY person in this world I've trusted with all of this. I can't continue to speak with you if you don't even trust in me and believe what I say…

Goodbye Joel, goodbye EMJO…

Emily

p.s. Hiding treats under the BATHROOM sink? Gross!

• •

Date: March 26, 2005 **Time:** 9:21 p.m. CST.
To: Elockhardt@wryword.comp
From: JoelJin@surftwn.comp
Subject: *Re: Nightmare that's real!*

Hey, sorry Emily. OF COURSE I BELIEVE YOU!!!! Why do you think I haven't been able to sleep much? I was HOPING you were kidding around, because it's just so bad! I don't want you to have to go through this. I'd rather it be anybody but you—I'd rather it be ME almost. I can't stand hearing how you're suffering. E-mail me back and at least tell me if last night was okay. PLEASE! You're my best friend, Em, and you always will be.

It hurts me when you hurt. I hate you hurting. Everything hurts. I guess it didn't help that I ate a dozen Chockoroos. Man my belly hurts. I burped a huge one and Janice started yelling for mom, saying that I had rancid cookie breath. (What does rancid mean?) I had to give her a whole box of the stash just to shut her up. She pigged five of them down in seconds and didn't even care that they came from under the bathroom sink. What kind of *girl* is that? I hate her.

Forgive me.
Joel

• •

Date: March 28, 2005 **Time:** 9:43 a.m. CST.
To: JoelJin@surftwn.comp
From: Elockhardt@wryword.comp
Subject: *I might forgive you*

I guess if it were you instead of me, I'd be hoping you were kidding too…so I guess I forgive you. I *need* to forgive you Joel. The night before last night was fine. I figured I'd let you stew a while in your own chockoroo juice. Ew. I do need you, Joel. I need your friendship…more than anything right now…It's bad, Joel. Things are real bad—and after last night, I don't feel safe anywhere in this house.

Before I went to bed, I checked my room—high and low—for that bug book and was relieved to have found nothing. I was so relieved, I almost cried. The first part of the night was fine. I actually SLEPT…'til about three thirty. That's when I heard the knock at my bedroom door. I ignored it, turning over and burying my head under the covers. But the rapping grew louder—and then it stopped. I don't know how I knew it, but I knew it: they were busy trying to turn the doorknob.

I got out of bed and raced for the door, but it was too late. The door came open and I was bathed in flies. They must have flung their horrific individual bodies against my door at the same time to make it knock—and used a collective effort to open the door.

Joel, these weren't houseflies—they were…*horseflies.* They were HUGE, and they bit me on every bit of exposed skin and right through my pajamas.

Remember last summer when you came up with us to the cabin and you got bit while swimming by just one of them? You had tears in your eyes, Joel. I was bitten by hundreds of them. Hundreds. ALL AT ONCE. The buzzing was so loud; I still have ringing in my ears right now. I don't know how I managed to move, but I think it's because even though most of me was scared, part of me was mad. And it was that part that led me down the hall, (covered in horseflies)…to where they were swarming from: under Bud's door. Even with all the racket from the flies, I could hear Bud snoring. I knew

I had to find that book in order to stop them. Don't ask me how…I just knew.

My hands were so swollen from all those bites that I couldn't feel much—I had to use both of them on either side just to turn the knob. I fell forward then…landing on Bud's bedroom floor. He was still snoring. The buzzing was still deafening. I mean there are zillions of horseflies thick as soup around him, plus a person drops like a dead redwood six feet away and still he snores…

I yelled for him to wake up—a couple of times—and finally he said something typical like, *"Huh? What?"* and sat up in bed. My Mom had no problem hearing me topple and called out for me.

She mumbled something like "What's going on, Em? Are you on the floor again?"

I yelled out to Mom that I was just using the bathroom and was fine.

Joel, as soon as those flies heard her voice? All of them—the ones that were covering me and the ones that were just buzzing over Bud, disappeared. But this time—even in the darkness I saw (sensed?) where they went.

The Bug book was lying open on Bud's desk and I watched, open-mouthed, as they all flew in there, good thing, I guess, because there was a fly buzzing in my throat that flew up and out then as well.

Yes, Joel…I watched them fly back inside the pages of a book. Bud didn't see it. He was too busy rubbing his eyes and yelling at me to get out of his room. I sprung up from the carpet, peering close at the pages and actually saw them "take their places," in the picture—like they were models or living mannequins. Quickly, I slammed it shut, turning it upside down on the desk. The back cover looked safe in the dark. It looked green and (except for the bar code at the bottom), blank.

Guess what Joel? Guess what? Lots of bugs are green, Joel. It wasn't blank. It wasn't blank at all…

chapter Four

To: JoelJin@surftwn.comp
From: Elockhardt@wryword.comp *(Continued)*

Bud was still half-asleep—he basically slept through the whole thing. I couldn't believe it. I felt him staring at me in the darkness. He didn't say anything for the longest time—it was weird. Finally he whispered my name and his bare feet hit the floor right next to his smelly, worn out slippers. He stepped over them without looking down.

He wanted to know what I was doin' in his room…in the middle of the night and I didn't know what to say.

Should I tell him the truth? Did he know what those bugs in his crazy book have been doing to me? Before I could reply, Bud walked towards me and felt my forehead with the palm of his hand. Bud felt my forehead? Whoa…

He was getting upset and asked me if I was getting sick. He told me I didn't feel warm, but that I'd been actin' so darn *strange* that he could tell something was definitely wrong. Bud shook my shoulders and told me I was freaking him out and that I'd better tell him what's up, now!

I started to blubber about horseflies and millipedes and fire ants…and Joel, of course. I made absolutely no sense whatsoever. Then something happened between Bud and me

21

that had never, ever happened before. Without a sound he took my hand and led me back to my room. I crawled into bed and he covered me up and stared down at me with a look I'd never seen from him before. It took me a moment before I realized what it was. It was the look of PITY, Joel. My brother, the kid who consistently forgets to floss and wears mismatched mittens to school was looking at *me* with *pity*. Just like the way Mom looks at that woman at the corner store holding that sign begging for food.

Bud then turned and walked toward my door, and I wanted to yell out something like, "Don't you dare pity me. Don't you know what's been happening here? How can you not see it?" but I didn't. I could only just whisper, "Watch out Bud."

He turned toward me and shook his head. He walked out, shutting my bedroom door behind him, and I began to cry. I must have cried for a while, 'cause I looked horrible this morning. My eyes were all bloodshot and puffy and you're not going to believe this, but I didn't even care. I, Emily Lockhardt, didn't care that I looked completely *ishy*—bordering on unattractive, even. Oh, Joel! Look what those bugs are doing to me.

I made it to school…barely. I didn't have the energy to do much at all—I got out of gym just by asking. Mr. Zealoust took one look at me and told me to go take it easy. I didn't even confront the ancient mean one about the bug report. I couldn't even mention bugs.

When I got home today Bud was at basketball practice and Mom and Dad were still at work—but it was still light out—daytime—and for some reason, I thought I'd be safe. Good ol' Em—playing the fool once again. I got a glass of milk and dug out some Santa Christmas cookies I'd hidden in the back of the freezer. There was very little left of the jolly fellows that were recognizable. No matter. I barely tasted them. I felt like a zombie, which was fine since I looked like a zombie. It took all the strength I had just to open the dishwasher.

I was rinsing my glass when I heard the chirping. I flinched. No, not now. Not in broad daylight. This isn't fair! I was actually muttering out loud.

Sure, Em. Like it's completely fair for the bugs to attack you at night...Huh?

Joel, I think I might be going off the deep end, because... I marched right up to Bud's room. The door was shut like always. The chirping was as loud as a hot, July night outside the cabin.

As if hypnotized, I had to see inside. I mean had to! My palm closed around the knob. Just as I turned it and pushed, the front door burst open and I heard Bud's familiar footsteps stomp across the kitchen linoleum.

Looking across the threshold was a scene that could have come from biblical times. I literally could not take it all in. I felt like my brain was about to go on strike.

I screamed for Bud to come upstairs. His room was completely covered in locusts, Joel. Some were as large as hot dogs! They hung from the ceiling light, Bud's poster of that cinnamon girl poster—everywhere. They covered his bed— making for a quivering green quilt. But the most amazing thing was they ignored me. They were too busy eating—yes, I said *eating*—everything in sight. Bud's bookcase that he'd crammed with all kinds of comic books, was now almost ½ empty. All that remained of the cinnamon girl was her right ear. I stood in that doorway, paralyzed, completely disgusted, yet fascinated, and it wasn't until I heard Bud call my name from the stairs that I was able to tear my eyes away. The locusts cocked their heads, then quickly they flew to the back cover in one, huge, greenish swoop. Bud, wearing a ripped sweatshirt and that stupid bandana around his neck, sauntered up the stairs and grinned.

What now? He mumbled, his mouth full of apple. He got a glimpse of the mess that had once been his room and the bright red fruit fell to the floor. Joel, the top blanket—you know, the one with the goofy cartoon character that he's had since he was five—was almost completely eaten off of the bed.

Bud pushed me aside and ran into what was left of his room. He grabbed me by the shoulders, grilling me, asking what happened over and over. He wanted to know what I had done to cause this. He dropped his arms and slowly turned around in a circle, surveying the damage.

"Not me, the locusts, Bud," I said to him and pointed to his desk. I told him that they came from that horrible book.

He picked up the shreds of what used to be his t-shirt, shook his head and told me I had crossed the line, that I had to get help. Something about how it was way beyond normal, even for me.

We heard Mom calling up from the kitchen.

I was frantic. I told Bud I couldn't believe he'd ever think I could have done this. I ran to him, grabbed his hand and led him to the desk where that horrible book lay.

Here! I said, picking it up and waving it in front of Bud. I told him it was that book—these bugs—that are the culprits not me.

I pressed my index finger so hard upon those hairy, disgusting, bodies I think I sprained it. Mom called out again. I jumped. I told Bud that something about this book is evil—

possessed—whatever you want to call it—all I know is that the insects in here are able to COME OUT! Of course Bud shook his head in disbelief. I grabbed his arms and shook as hard as I could.

I had to get through to him. I told him I couldn't believe he hadn't seen something—heard something—anything strange with that book. Bud's eyes looked glassy. He pulled away and sat on the edge of what used to be his blanket. Mom called again, and we heard her start up the stairs.

Bud sprung into action. He grabbed me and pulled me out of his room. The door slammed behind us just as Mom came upon the landing.

She was exasperated, saying stuff like, "Well, there you are!" Then she told Bud that Michael Williams had called for him and asked her if Bud was feeling better? Uh-oh. Mom was on a roll. She asked him, "What's going on? Did you go hightailing into the woods again? Bud, what's wrong, why did you leave basketball practice early? Are you sick?" All that stuff. She reached for the doorknob of his bedroom and told him that maybe he should lie down.

"No!" Bud and I yelled out at the same time. Thinking quickly, Bud seized her hand and pulled it into his own. He told her that he couldn't possibly lie down. He had way too much energy for that. He then said he was thinking he'd start cleaning his room and the garage—right now.

Mom looked shocked. I did too. She and Dad had been buggin' Bud to clean the garage since summer. Her hand flew to his forehead.

"Are you sure you're okay?" She asked him. Bud grinned and told her he was better than okay, adding that he was great…now. He placed his palm on his belly and said he probably shouldn't have eaten six tacos for lunch…Mom looked skeptical at first, then Bud burped. She "tsked" and thankfully, grinned.

She turned her sights on me asking if I was okay. She said I looked so very pale. *Well, gee, that's what happens, Mom, when you have the daylights scared out of you.*

Bud quickly said, "Em? She's always whiter than white, Maw. Our own snow leopard." He raised his arms over me and bared his teeth.

Mom laughed and went into her room to get ready for her evening out. After we heard her bedroom door shut, we went back into Bud's room. He locked the door behind us, then crossed to the desk and picked up the Bug book.

"Well, I guess I should have guessed," he said to me, staring at the yucky thing in his hand.

"Should have guessed what?" I asked, my stomach churning.

Finally, Bud opened up to me. He told me that he could of sworn he heard something…buzzing when he held it for the first time. Bud's eyes scanned his demolished room. Once, he even thought he felt it…vibrate he admitted. He tossed the book on his dresser and threw his hands in the air. "But I figured I'd just imagined it," Bud said softly, "I had to have imagined it right?"

I shook my head *no*.

Bud admitted that he'd felt weird about the book all along. He said that Peter Schwann, that goofy, kind of chubby kid from school gave him the book. He said Peter had told him that the book was so real it was freaking him out. Peter had said they were still after him now, and he had to run. He said it was cursed. Bud said he didn't believe him, of course. He knows that Peter has always been dramatic—and full of baloney.

Bud burped again. Tacos and Bud do not mix. (Sound familiar, Chokoroos boy?) Scowling, I asked him how Peter got the book in the first place.

Bud told me that some weird, hairy teenager approached Peter outside the nature store at the Mall of America. The dude asked Peter if he liked to read about the world of bugs. Of course Peter said, "yeah."

He said the weird guy grinned so wide it looked like his lips met his ears and his teeth were a gross, greenish gray. Then the guy shoved it at Peter and told him to keep it. Peter said the weirdo said something like, "This book is out of this world."

The guy laughed so hard after that, Bud said that it even made Peter nervous, and then the strange dude scampered off.

Bud told me that that Peter said this guy looked like nothing he'd ever seen before—ever—almost not quite human. He said he half expected the dude to bypass the mall shuttle and hop a space ship.

By now, Bud's breathing was coming more rapidly. I reached atop his dresser, grabbed his inhaler and tossed it to him. He gave it a couple of puffs. His asthma had been greatly improving over the past few years. The doctor said he believed Bud would be one of those kids who might eventually grow out of it. But the craziness of the last few days wouldn't help with that.

I crossed to the bed and sat down beside him. Bud shook his head. He tossed the inhaler onto the dresser and ran his hands through his hair. His gaze dropped to the floor. Bud whispered that Peter didn't have the book for long before he said the spiders wanted him. He said they were following him.

27

Then Bud looked me directly in the eyes and told me that he didn't believe him. He thought he was teasing. He said, "Em, you know how much Peter likes to tease."

I nodded. Peter was one of those kids that tended to exaggerate things—*everything*, actually. He was kind of a loner at school and in the neighborhood and he often looked for attention by teasing anybody who would listen to him. Bud was just about the only person that he regularly talked to.

I asked Bud if Peter told him what sorts of things he saw and felt.

"Naw, not really," Bud said. He just told Bud that he didn't want the book anymore and to get rid of it or give it to Willy Dunkan.

You remember Willy Dunkan, don't you, Joel? Yes, he's still the biggest bully in school—he harasses Peter and a lot of other kids almost every day. I heard he even had to go to Juvenile Court this year for giving Peter a black eye. I asked Bud why Peter would want him to give the book to his arch nemesis. Bud threw his hands up in the air and said, "Em, take a look at what's left of my bedroom. Don't you see why?" Of course, I did.

"Well, that explains a lot," I said. Bud swallowed hard, looking even more frightened all of the sudden. He wiped his sweaty palms on his jeans and told me that there was something he had to tell me about Peter. Suddenly, I realized, I didn't want to know. I started for the door.

Bud called after me. "Em, I didn't see him at school today," he said, picking up the book and dropping it onto the floor. Bud said that he really hoped nothing had happened to him.

Oh, Joel, so do I!

chapter Five

To: JoelJin@surftwn.comp
From: Elockhardt@wryword.comp *(Continued)*

Joel, even with all I've gone through, I couldn't believe what Bud was saying. Where was Peter? Was he at their fort in the woods? Speaking of which, I never knew that Bud and Peter ever HAD a fort in the woods until a few weeks ago. Still, it explains where Bud was taking off to lately. Is the world going mad...or just us?

Bud and I talked about it and agreed that we couldn't tell the folks. Mainly because they wouldn't believe us. We sat in the living room, plotting what we had to do to get out of this mess.

Finally, we decided that we would throw the book away. Let those bugs be buried in some smelly landfill—where the book would get smurshed up—along with all of their disgusting bug bodies. We knew that we had to clean up Bud's room or Mom and Dad would think we had trashed it and they would go ballistic and we couldn't blame them either.

Bud and I used the huge leaf bags we had left from last fall and basically tossed what was left of his comic books, posters, strands of clothes that'd been left on the floor, and we even rolled up what was left of his blanket and crammed it inside the bag.

It was exhausting, but sheer fear kept us going. I felt like I was in some kind of fog and Bud said he felt just like the time he'd gotten the wind knocked out of him at football practice.

How weird it was to be working with Bud instead of against him! When we were done with the room, Bud lifted the book and forcibly slammed it back onto the desk. He said something like, "Take that you stupid, slimy slugs. I hope ya felt it."

Bud took a deep breath, then picked it back up and threw it onto the floor. The book flew open. I ran to grab it before the bugs could decide to come out. I clutched it shut and felt the book shudder. What was happening? How could a book shudder, Joel? I don't know how any of this is possible. It's stranger than strange. The book started vibrating—it's as if it was angry. My hands shaking, I showed it to Bud.

Bud grabbed the book from me and raced downstairs to the kitchen where he dropped it inside a small garbage bag, sealed it with a twisty tie, then put the whole thing inside a leaf bag, sealed that, and brought it to the curb.

Joel, when he walked back in, free from that horrible thing, he looked so…relieved that I started to laugh. He just stared at me at first, but then he started laughing too.

"Is it over now?" I asked my brother. "Is it really done with?"

Bud said something like, "Of course it's over." He looked worried again for a second and then, as if reaching for some inner optimism, he threw his hands up in the air and whistled the theme to Rocky.

We then got lame and lamer. I said something like, "Gee Bud, I'll try not to BUG you so much for now on." Even though the "joke" was so dumb tears were stinging my eyes and my ribs ached. We sat there together in the kitchen for a long time sometimes making lame jokes, sometimes not—right up until my parents got home. Dad wanted to know what was up with all the garbage out on the curb, and he was eyeing Bud suspiciously. Bud was quick on his feet. He told dad that before he started on the garage he'd decided to clean his room. The folks looked so surprised, I giggled.

Bud grinned his loopy lopsided grin and said that all that cleaning had tuckered him out…

"Tuckered?" Mom and Dad echoed.

Bud shrugged and yawned. He said he'd better head on up to bed. Then he leaned down and whispered to me: what's *left* of it anyway. Ha!

I lost a couple drops of milk through my nose on that one. The folks had no clue what had gotten into us, but they were happy we were laughing instead of fighting.

Mom handed me a tissue, tapped me on the nose and told me to head up, too. I told her I'd be up in ten minutes…that was an hour ago.

I'm glad she and Dad went to play cards tonight—that always poops 'em out—so I'm sure they're "z'ing" as I write this.

Joel, I am so relieved that this is OVER! I still feel edgy—but I think that's probably normal, don't you?

Em

• •

Date: March 28, 2005 **Time:** 9:46 p.m. CST.
To: Elockhardt@wryword.comp

From: JoelJin@surftwn.comp
Subject: *Re: I might forgive you*

Heck yeah that's normal. Remember I told you that *I'm* having trouble sleeping just hearing about all of this.

I'm proud of you Em. You not only are a dead-ringer for Jessica Simpson (as you indicated in your side-by-side photo comparison you sent over the net), but you've got the bravery of some sort of ninja broad buried deep within, too. And whaddya know? Bud's moved up a few notches on my "I'm impressed" scale, too. Sort of. Hey wasn't Peter Schwann the husky dude who knocked the wind out of Bud? Weird.

With all you've gone through these last few days you guys should have your own sitcom called something like "Quit Bugging Me!" Stupid title, eh?

Man, I am glad it's over. I haven't had much of an appetite since all this started ('cept for Chokoroos) and Mom has noticed something's warped. She sees me sitting here all frantic n' waiting for your e-mails, only to more frantically read them, then frantically pace and pull my hair spikes higher. All this frantic stuff is driving her crazy. She told me I need to broaden my horizons and learn how to surf or something. "You're not in MN anymore," she tells me. I tell her I can barely walk, let alone try and balance on a slippery board above shark-infested waters. When I explained to her that you were having the usual trouble with Bud, that seemed to ease her mind a little—but she can tell that's not all of it.

Listen Em, let's get back to our boring, everyday life. I can hardly wait to hear from you about normal stuff. Ya know, gossiping about the kids at school and digging up dirt on your brother—you will still hate Bud, at least sorta, right? I can't imagine that stopping completely. Why, that would be like me not hating the Queen of Mean. Speaking of which, I never noticed how much she looks like Cher until now. She sure as heck is tall enough. And that long, dark hair, the snooty sneer—she could take it on the road. All she needs is to learn how to sing on key. Righto. Like that'll ever happen.

Hey Janice just came up behind me a few minutes ago and started reading your e-mail. I screamed for her to get away or I'd tell Joseph Julig about the rash of zits on her legs. She's out of here! All she made out was that you guys have a problem with bugs. She thinks you have a normal problem that an exterminator would take care of. Funny, huh? An exterminator…

That stuff about that Peter kid is way creepy. I don't wanna think about it…Say—what's Bud going to say to your folks about his room? I mean, won't they notice that all his comic books and stuff are awol? Mine sure would. They notice everything. They think it's their duty or something. Hey, Bud could tell them that he finally decided he was too old for that kiddie blanket (duh! can't believe he was still using it anyway) and that he had outgrown most of the comic-book life, too. That'd probably work. He is getting older you know, Em. When I called you last week, I almost didn't recognize his voice—I thought it was your Dad for a second. Sounds like his face is clearing up even.

Anyway, this bug stuff is way too warped. Em, I don't mind telling you, I've been feeling WAY too creepy lately. You know, being a guy and all, I never used to mind bugs, but now, now I could never see a bee again and that would be sweet as honey for me. Speaking of which, I'm sure glad you didn't ever turn to the mosquito page. Can you imagine? Being stung by zillions of those buggers?

Uh-oh, Janice is back. She's flipping her hair around and pretending she has no interest in what I'm writing. Yeah, right. Now she's got her shins out and she's yelling at me. When did she get so tan? Never noticed that before. California sunshine has its perks when it comes to shins. Yes, I see. I have to admit, they have cleared up a bit, darn it. Anyway, Em, we're definitely driving her nutsier. It's a good thing you reminded me to erase your e-mails. The Queen of Mean would have devoured them if she could. She's right behind me now...Boy, she's being quiet—as you know, that's almost impossible for her. Good—she just left the room and she was whistling. Janice whistling? I don't trusPOGJ*)(p

A spider just dropped on my head and hit the key board. It's happening here to me Em! It's hap)OK)O(_{

chapter Six

Date: March 28, 2005 **Time:** 9:58 p.m. CST.
To: Elockhardt@wryword.comp
From: JoelJin@surftwn.comp
Subject: *Re: I might forgive you*

Can a brother be charged with murdering his sister if she drove him buggy?

Guess where the spider came from? Man, she ticks me off! After Queen of Mean saw your e-mail and how freaked out I was she thought it'd be "funny" to capture a spider from the carport and drop it on me.

Unlike most girls, she's never been afraid of bugs. Remember in third grade when she put the shiny black beetle in my lunch box? If I weren't so freaked out from all of this, I'd already be plotting my revenge. She just isn't normal.

Man, that's strange about Peter. Hope he's okay. He's a strange guy, but a pretty decent guy. Anyway, I gotta go, Em. It's late and I still haven't done my math homework or tormented Janice. I'm glad your problem has finally been solved. REAL GLAD!

Joel

. . . .

Date: March 29, 2005 **Time:** 6:08 a.m. CST.
To: JoelJin@surftwn.comp
From: Elockhardt@wryword.com
Subject: *Freaked out!*

Joel, I can't believe I'm sitting here writing this. Truly, I'm not sure this isn't a dream. I know you aren't up now, (it being only 4 a.m. for you), but I didn't know what else to do, I'm hoping that at the very least you'll get up early and check your e-mail. You and your family ARE coming on the first, right? I didn't imagine that, too, did I? Did I??? I WILL see you in two days, right?

Oh Joel, I can't stand this. I can't! I mean, if Bud were… oh, I'd better start from the beginning or you'll never understand what happened. Right. As if I even do…

I read your e-mail and I must admit it brought back my memory of the true Janice. I'd forgotten just how abnormal she is. But believe it or not, that's not important now. Joel, I can't believe I'm writing this, but I don't think this is ever going to end.

Last night I practically crawled upstairs to bed; the weakness just seemed to hit me all at once. I was so happy to snuggle down and be able to really relax and shut my eyes. I fell asleep immediately and it seemed like only five minutes had passed when I heard it. But it actually had been hours. It was around two or so—I made myself sit up and look at the clock—hoping I was really just dreaming. I made myself get out of bed—STILL hoping I was just dreaming. Hoping against hope, that's all. I'd left my bedroom door open a crack and realized it was coming from down the hall.

It's hard to describe the sound I heard, but the closest thing I can say is that it reminded me of that Hitchcock movie, *The Birds*. Rustling…lots of rustling. It wasn't a

TV. It wasn't a flock of geese on the lawn. I knew it wasn't normal. I guess after you've been exposed to "un-normal" time and time again, it gets pretty easy to recognize. I knew in the pit of my stomach and in my wildly racing heart that they were back. I felt like I couldn't swallow properly. Like my throat was going on strike. I raced blindly toward my door—tripping over my slippers and landing about a foot away from the threshold.

The rustling grew louder and I crawled forward until I was close enough to get my hand up and slap the door shut. Kneeling, I quickly clicked the lock.

Then it hit me.

If they were back, was Bud okay? The way he slept, he probably hadn't even heard them yet. Joel, I felt so frightened, so defeated and so tired. How was this possible? We'd gotten rid of them, right?

I kept wondering if maybe I was dreaming. Maybe my dreams had just grown more real feeling because of all the trauma I'd been through—but I knew then as I know now, that's not the way it is. I heard some scratching sound outside my bedroom door. They were back and they wanted me to welcome them home. Whatever they were—this time. I had to open it. I had to. What if they were already attacking comatose Bud? And why didn't my parents hear them?

My knees were vibrating as I stood and unlocked the door. Slowly, I turned the knob and pulled. With everything I'd already seen, I figured it would take a whole lot to shock me.

Well, there *was* a whole lot to shock me. A whole lotta moths. They were frantically flying about covering the hall from floor to ceiling. It was like I was suddenly tossed into a vat of moth soup. Some were the brightest of white—almost blindingly white—while others wore incredible incandescent reds, yellows, greens, blues, and even purple. If you'd happen to see this on PBS or something, you'd suck in your breath at their beauty. Last night I did not feel particularly awestruck. Of course I was scared, but mostly…I was outraged. How did they get back in here? We threw them away. How was this possible?

I struggled to see anything through the thousands of batting wings and finally I glimpsed Bud's bedroom door…it was open! Covering my eyes and mouth, I barged through the swarm towards Bud's room. I felt the moths become tangled in my long, silky hair. Their bodies and wings flapping wildly in an attempt to escape.

Joel, you must understand that some of these moths were HUGE! I mean, their bodies were literally the size of softballs. When their wings slapped against my face I could feel my flesh tear and I could see my blood splattered on their bodies. But I kept moving—feeling the bodies of the moths squish into the carpet underneath my bare feet. It got pretty gooey and slimy and I guess that's what made me slip and my face was buried in their guts and flapping wings. When I went to talk, Joel, I could taste their innards that'd been smeared there.

I didn't care. Joel, me, *Emily Lockhardt*, the girl who used to freak out that your mutt, Scruffy had just licked her lips, had just unknowingly licked bug guts and DIDN'T CARE. All I could think about was getting to Bud. Nothing else mattered.

Desperately, I struggled to stand—only to slip back down again and again until finally, using the wall (and their bodies) I could get up—right inside the threshold of Bud's room. I was relieved to see just a few moths sputtering about by the window, the rest of his room was clear. I was shocked however, to see that the bed beneath the window was empty. I checked his closet, thinking maybe he'd run in there for cover—no luck. I even checked under his bed…nothing. Joel, the fear I felt then was almost unbearable. I started crying and calling out for him—softly, this time. I didn't want to wake Mom and Dad. There was no answer.

There was no answer because Bud was nowhere to be found. He was gone, Joel. *Gone*!

chapter Seven

To: JoelJin@surftwn.comp
From: Elockhardt@wryword.comp *(Continued)*

I was so upset; I guess I didn't hear them follow me into the room. Before I knew what was happening, the moths surrounded me and I actually felt my body lift up off the floor a few inches. Angry, I lurched forward and they dropped me. That wasn't the end, Joel. Once again they took their "places" and began to rise, taking me with them. It was so bizarre. I was "flying" with them, and I knew they wanted to take me somewhere…somewhere where I probably couldn't get back. I tried to bat them away, but there were too many of them and I wound up about two feet off the ground—zooming towards the hall.

Even though my arms were smothered in their flapping bodies, I managed to grab onto the doorframe and I held on using every bit of strength I had. They were just too much for me, Joel. Way too large and way too strong, and as I felt my fingers slipping I started crying—and I mean crying—and I swear I heard them snicker. Moths *giggling*? Yes. I hated them even more then and I couldn't stand it. I was so frightened; I kicked out and screamed for Dad and Bud's door slammed shut.

His familiar cough and footsteps followed, and the startled moths dropped me to the floor as the horrible creatures flew off down the stairs.

Dad whispered, "Em, this is getting to be a habit with you, isn't it," as he came out into the hall, his dark brown hair standing every which way—his glasses clutched in his hand.

He stuck them on his face and reached down and grabbed me under my shoulders. As he was pulling me up he asked me, "What's wrong? What was going on?"

I knew I couldn't tell him the truth, because I couldn't prove a darn thing. For whatever reason those bugs did it they wouldn't—or couldn't—do it around adults.

So I told Dad I'd had a nightmare and must have been sleepwalking. Because of my strange behavior recently, and the fact that I had never sleepwalked before, I knew Dad sensed that something was truly wrong.

He was tired, though, and I hugged him and told him that everything was okay, and that we both needed to get back to bed and he finally agreed. He started back towards his bedroom but then quickly whirled around.

He said that I'd been very loud and asked me why didn't Bud wake up—or did he? He asked reaching for Bud's bedroom door.

I slapped his hand away and told him to leave him sleep. I said Bud was fine and reminded him that Bud snores through hurricanes.

My Dad nodded (even though there aren't any hurricanes in Minnesota) and thankfully went into his bedroom and shut the door.

I raced downstairs looking for Bud. Where had those moths taken him? Flicking on lights as I went, I searched for my brother. I checked the living room, the dining room, the kitchen and even the yucky cellar. Nothing. No Bud. No sign of Bud. The glaring lights seemed to taunt me saying, "See? Your brother's gone. All gone. No matter how many lights you turn on, you'll never find him…because he's *gone*!"

Where was he? What should I do? I dropped down, sitting in the middle of the kitchen linoleum, my head in my hands. I knew I'd have to tell Mom and Dad that Bud was missing. Whether they believed me about "who" took him or not, he was missing and I needed help. I rose, defeated and scared, and started for the stairs.

It was then I felt the cool air rustle my face and hair. I swirled around and saw the curtains on the patio door rise up the slightest bit. I raced over flinging the curtains back to see that the door was open. About three feet open—far enough for Bud to have gotten through…wide enough for the moths to have carried him through.

I ran to the front hall closet pulling on my boots, (not bothering to tie them) and threw on the first coat I found.

Saying a silent prayer, I came upon the patio doors and stopped. *Where to now?* My eyes scanned the melting snow. It's not like the moths would have left any tracks. I walked out into the freezing night (I felt as if I were stepping into a huge black mouth), and whispered Bud's name. Nothing.

I stepped off of the deck, my boots crunching the snow, my breath soaring heavenward in the cold late winter air.

Again I called his name, only this time a little louder than before. Nothing. I looked under the deck and saw only familiar shadows. Why hadn't I grabbed a flashlight? I crept across the back lawn, my eyes searching the frozen ground for any sign of my brother.

Underneath our old swing set was where I saw it. It was stretched out and dingy. It was Bud's sock...but nothing else. I picked it up, clutching it to my chest. I got the biggest lump in my throat; I thought I wasn't going to be able to draw another breath. I stood there holding Bud's sock, telling myself that everything was going to be okay, until I was finally able to swallow.

Joel, then I knew that Bud and I were involved in something extremely dangerous. I thought too how Bud had told me that the real reason we couldn't tell Mom and Dad about the bug book was because it had some sort of a curse on it. A kind of curse that children could experience and even die from but that adults were unable to see or be affected by. That was the most frightening aspect of it all.

Still, there I was, outside in the freezing night, alone. What was I going to do about Bud? I headed back towards the house to get the folks (I felt I had to), and that's when I heard it. It was coming from the garage...

I clomped across the snow and ice frantically searching the ground for the sound. Nothing. I didn't hear anything else and saw no sign of my brother—not even his other sock. I stood there for the longest time, and just as I decided I'd have to go back inside and get Mom and Dad, I heard it again. It was a snorty kind of sound really. The kind of sound one makes when somebody is quietly sleeping, then suddenly takes a huge breath. The kind of obnoxious sound like Bud makes when he's sleeping. My pulse danced. It WAS Bud's snort. It had to be. I was sure I recognized it. There was no sign of him though. Where was he? Thankfully, yet another familiar snore followed, and I realized the sound was coming from above me. I looked up, willing my eyes to see through the darkness. There was his familiar bony form, all curled up—way up-there. Bud was sleeping on the garage roof! The moths must have dumped him there when Dad surprised me. They were really flying high with Bud. I guess I realized by now that these bugs work together.

How was I going to get Bud off the roof? Joel, he was sleeping like a baby by now, snoring away in his own little la la land.

I called his name softly, so as not to wake my parents. Yeah, right, like that would wake up Bud. I then thought of using the rocks around the house as a nudge to rouse him. I missed him more than I hit him, but the one that bonked him right in the middle of the forehead did the trick.

He sat up, rubbing his eyes like usual, only this time, he'd looked around and then rubbed them again.

I told him he was outside and that he needed to come down because he was on the garage roof.

Bud was really out of it. "Huh?" he muttered, saying "How did I get up on the roof?" Suddenly he remembered how.

Bud eyes grew huge. He mumbled that they were back. The bugs are back!

I shook my head and plucked out part of a moth wing that had been wedged between my front teeth and told him to tell me something I didn't know…Bud walked to the edge of the roof then lowered his lanky frame down, dropping the last few feet into the snow below.

I grabbed his arm and we ploughed through the snow for the back door and we almost made it inside. Almost is *never* close enough.

We looked up and saw the silhouettes of Mom and Dad in the threshold of our patio. Mom's hands were cemented to her hips. She started to speak then stopped (shaking her head), then finally blurted out something parenty like, "What in heaven's name are you two doing outside in your jammies in the middle of the night? Bud—you know darn well that the cold could easily exacerbate your asthma! What's wrong with you two?" *You get the gist.*

Bud and I quickly looked at each other. Every part of my body was quivering. I was not EmJo, but Jell-O. We were SO caught!

chapter Eight

To: JoelJin@surftwn.comp
From: Elockhardt@wryword.comp *(Continued)*

The look they gave us Joel…it could have been funny—but it wasn't—they were too mad. Mom's hair was sticking out all over the place and her face was redder than ours. She seemed like she was going to burst. Dad just glared at us, stomping his bare feet on the linoleum over and over. Bud and I were trapped—right outside the door on the deck—right in front of our tired, shocked parents.

Finally Dad spoke. He yelled out, "Buderick James Lockhardt! (Uh-oh, complete names…) blah, blah, blah, why, in heaven's name, blah, blah, would your mother and I find you outside in the middle of the night—in your pajamas, without a coat or…he looked down, or boots…or…*a sock*?" Dad asked Bud if he was MAD at his right foot and punishing it by giving it frostbite? "Good question, Dad," Bud said.

Bud, looking guilty as heck stared down at his cherry red toes and shrugged.

Mom moved closer, eyed me up and down and then said, between clenched teeth, "*Emily, Emily, Emily* (uh-oh, the dreaded triple name repetition), why, blah, blah, in heaven's name, are you outside in the middle of the blah, blah, blah

46

night with Bud?" And then she asked me, tilting her head to the side, why I decided to wear my father's coat? Oops. I looked down at the woolen cloak that hung clear to my ankles. No wonder it'd felt so heavy. I hadn't noticed I was wearing it before. I shrugged too.

There we were, Bud shivering, and me sweating. I guess we must have made an interesting picture.

Bud then said it was kinda cold out there, and asked if we could come inside. By now he was dancing from one frozen foot to the sockless other.

"Good Lord, yes, yes, for crying out loud get in here!" Dad said, stepping out of the way so we could quickly pass into the warmth of the kitchen.

Mom grabbed Bud's hand and marched him upstairs, "You get out of those cold, wet clothes and get a sock on!" she ordered. Bud laughed at her one-sock remark. Mom just said, "Move it, mister!" and swatted his 16-year-old rear.

So, that meant for the moment, it was Dad and me alone. I stood there swaddled in his long coat and my untied boots, afraid to say or do anything that might push him over the edge. I recall wondering what the temperature was inside the house. I was dripping wet with sweat. Was it ninety degrees? 100? All of the sudden, I felt really sick to my stomach and kind of dizzy. I really wanted to sit down. I needed to sit down but I was afraid to move.

"Okay, Emily," Dad said to me, scratching his head and frowning. "First," he goes, "I find you screaming in the hall upstairs, now I find you and your brother outside in the middle of the night blah, blah." Dad was looming over me shaking his tired, mad and confused head. I craned my neck to look up into his eyes. I could see now why he was nick-named Swish in college. He really IS tall, isn't he? Those other basketball players didn't stand a chance when he was near the net. Funny, the things that pop out at you at the strangest times. Like the veins in Dad's neck as he started drumming his fingers on the table, tap, tap, tap. Over and over and over again. Tap, tap, tapety tap. Ack! Finally he asked me what the heck was going on with me. What was I trying to hide?

He said this was all just too bizarre—especially for me—but this was *really* strange, even for Bud! He pulled one of the dining table chairs out and dropped upon it. I was envious of his reclining position—I was still boiling hot and frozen in the exact same spot. I felt way dizzier now, and unbelievably warm. In fact, I saw a couple of "Dad's" swimming before me.

"Well?" He demanded, shaking his head and folding his arms across his chest. "What the heck were you two doing out there?"

Joel, I just couldn't come up with anything to say.

So I mumbled, "Um, I, um, we, um, were, um, Dad? I don't feel good…"

He said something like, "Yeah, I BET you don't." All of the sudden, next thing I know, I'm lying on the couch in the living room.

"What happened? Where's Bud?" I asked sitting up.

"Bud's in the kitchen with your Father, eating French toast. You fainted," my Mom said, removing the washcloth that had been across my forehead.

"And no wonder," she continued, rinsing it out in the bowl on the coffee table and slapping it back on with an alarming amount of vigor, "what with you and your cohort, gallivanting outdoors in the frigid winter night."

Uh-oh. I'd forgotten about that. I lay back down. What had Bud told them? Did he tell them about the bug book? Did he make something up? My mind raced with questions.

"Bud," I called out weakly. Nothing. I lurched up. "Bud. Get your butt in here!" I screeched. Soon he was standing by the couch, wiping syrup off his chin with the sleeve of his flannel shirt.

"Hey, Em. Feelin' better?" he asked. I nodded yes, searching his face for some sign. Had he spilled the beans? Had he? Bud winked.

He told Mom that he thought I could use some of her hot chocolate…She leaped up to get me some.

I whispered to Bud that I knew they must have cross-examined him about why we were outside. What did he tell them? Did he tell them the truth? Bud grinned and plopped on the edge of the couch, bouncing me up and down in the process.

He told me he couldn't tell them the truth. They'd never believe us, because of that curse, and we'd never be able to show them—or prove it.

I nodded sadly.

Bud admitted that at first he'd panicked and couldn't think of anything to say—plus, he said under his breath, we were all—I mean they were worried about you…

I smiled—Bud was worried about *me*….

Bud told me then that something happened that was like a miracle or something—the greatest lie just…came to him. He grinned broadly and ran a hand through his dark blonde hair. His green eyes were sparkling.

He said he realized they hadn't seen him on the garage roof, thank heavens, so he said he thought he'd heard Tommy's lab, Dixie, wailing beneath his window.

What a great idea! Bud had been moaning all week about Tommy's dog running away. And Dixie came over all the time. Bud said that Dad believed him saying something like, "Well, as attached to the mutt as you are, that explains you parading outside, but what about Em?" Bud's grin broadened as he repeated what he'd said.

"I told Mom and Dad that you heard me thumping down the stairs, and came to investigate," said Bud, adding that he reminded them what a snoop I am and that I always hear everything. Bud couldn't help it. He started laughing. He said that Dad believed him and told Bud that he'd already seen you upstairs in the hall—that you had said you'd been sleepwalking.

My face burned with the lies. How lame an excuse it seemed in the light of the dawning day.

"Anyway," Bud continued, "I told them that once you got outside we both searched for Dixie—but no luck…"

I asked Bud if they asked him why he hadn't put on his coat or shoes and Bud grinned again.

He said they had and that he had looked at them real solemn and said, 'By the time I'd gotten them on, Dixie could have been gone.' Bud said the folks just looked at each other, rolling their eyes. Bud HAD always been attached to that stinky mutt and nobody really gets why. That mangy thing always smells like rotten saurkraut.

My brother then told me that this was one time where all his past nitwit behavior came in very handy. He looked so proud. Joel, I had to hand it to Bud. I told him that I never thought I'd admit it but…he wasn't as completely stupid as I thought he was.

Bud pretended he was deaf. What did you say? He asked me. That your brother is brilliant with a *capital z*? I started to laugh and thonked him in his side. He clutched his chest and keeled off the couch landing flat on his back on the living room plush.

"You killed him," my Mom said flatly while handing me my hot chocolate. She asked, "Who is taking out the garbage?"

Bud and Mom grinned, but the mere mention of garbage brought me right back to our horrible buggy reality. The Bug Book. We had thrown it in the garbage and it didn't go away! It came back with a vengeance, and it was still out there somewhere. Somewhere close. And I knew that Bud and I had to find it soon…before it found us.

Em

chapter Nine

Date: March 29, 2005 **Time:** 7:23 a.m. CST.
To: Elockhardt@wryword.comp
From: JoelJin@surftwn.comp
Subject: *Re: Freaked out!*

Yeah I did get up early—it's been pretty easy to do that lately—since I wake up in the middle of the night and lay there anyway. Yes, Em, I'll be there day after tomorrow. Finally, timing worked out for us, huh? We deserve it—and some good ol' Minnesota hotdish. But, Emily—moths lifting Bud out of his bed? Out of the house? You're right, you MUST find that book. Em, I've been thinking…who is the author of that book? What's the dude's name? Why am I assuming it's a guy? Well, what sort of girl would do something like that? Besides Janice I mean. I dunno. I can't imagine any-body who would do something like that. Hey, now that I'm thinking about it, who is the publisher? Maybe there would be some clue there though I dunno what.

You know, when you wrote that Bud had dumped the book in the garbage, I wondered about whether it would all end so easy. I mean, if those things are able to slither out from the pages of a book and terrorize you guys what's to stop them from chewing their way out of a couple of plastic bags? I know, I know, looking back now doesn't help at all, and I guess I should have told you what I was thinking, but I just wanted your nightmare to be over so much that I hoped that they would die in that garbage heap and rot in the landfill.

But Em, how were the bugs able to actually move the book, and where is the book now? I'm hoping by the time I read your e-mail tonight, you will have found the book and figured out how to get rid of it once and for all. If not, I'm will be wracking my brain all day—trying to come up with something—something for you to do to insure that they will be gone forever.

Janice is up. She's sticking her tongue out at me and pouring milk over her gross fiber yucky granola crap at the same time. Yeah, morning to you too Queen of Mean. You'll be happy to know she's got a HUGE red zit on the end of her nose and it's getting ready to BLOW!!! SWEET!

Look for that book Em. You gotta find it! E-mail me as soon as you can.

Joel

PS How can you tell rotten sauerkraut from normal? CAN sauerkraut get any more rotten than normal?

• •

Date: March 29, 2005 **Time:** 9:36 a.m. CST.
To: JoelJin@surftwn.comp
From: Elockhardt@wryword.comp
Subject: *Re: Freaked out!*

Okay get this: Almost unbelievably, Bud and I both "felt warm" according to Mom, and we were both told to stay home from school. I think she was just worried about the way we were acting and wanted to keep an eye on us. But thankfully, she had a bunch of "Save Our Park" committee stuff to do and she took off about nine. So, Bud and I immediately bundled up (his foot is only a little bit frostbit), and went in search of our greatest nightmare.

We found the book. It was under Dad's workbench in the garage. It was beneath a bunch of tools and maps. Joel, I think it was actually trying to hide from us.

I don't know what made Bud look in there—I never would have—but we'd already scanned the entire yard—and Bud "had a feeling," that the book was in the garage. He was right.

The book was open when we found it. Two full, glossy pages of killer bees stared out at Bud and I quickly snapped it shut. My fear must of telegraphed Bud with my eyes.

Bud told me not to worry, that the stupid little bees couldn't survive in this cold. "That much even *I* know," he'd said.

I shivered and checked the old thermometer Dad had hanging over the workbench. Thirty degrees. Freezing. Yes! For once I was actually grateful to be living in the Minnesota tundra.

Bud held the book so hard his fingers were white, and we just stood there, staring at each other. But, what do we do now? We certainly couldn't throw the book away…again. We'd already learned the hard way that they were very resourceful and very frightening.

Let's look around and see if we can come up with a way to squish all of these bugs from hell! Bud said, his eyes already scanning the dank garage. The wind howled and it took all the strength I had not to join in.

I wondered aloud if this was too big—too much for us to handle…I sat down on an overturned crate in the corner of the garage, draping my arm over Dad's hibachi.

"Wake up, Em," Bud said to me angrily. "We don't have a choice. We either get rid of them, before…" I remember feeling like I was going to hurl. I said, "before what? Bud. Before what?"

Joel, if you'd seen Bud's face then…the way his eyes darted around, refusing to look at me…I knew we were in grave danger. Now I understand what "grave" danger means. It means you're probably headed to your own grave. But even understanding all that, I had to hear Bud say it.

"Before they get rid of us, right Bud?" I said to him. He was facing the other way and I yelled his name again 'til he finally whirled around and screamed,

"YES, EM! THAT'S RIGHT! WE GOTTA FIGURE OUT HOW TO GET RID OF THIS THING BEFORE IT GETS RID OF US!!!!"

Suddenly, in spite of Bud's outburst I felt calm. I knew we were in this together. I closed my eyes, willing myself to think of a foolproof way to kill the book. *Kill a book*? Is this unbelievable, or what? Rhythmically, I tapped the tiny barbecue.

Bud saw me and squealed, "That's it!" He raced over to me.

I kept saying, "What? What?" I lurched up. Bud's eyes were shining as he said, "The barbecue, Em." He started jumping up and down saying he couldn't believe he didn't think of it before…

"Think of what before? Dinner?" I asked Bud how he could even think of eating at a time like this? Bud shook his head.

55

I'll never forget what he said. It was pretty clever, Joel. He said, "Em, we're going to barbecue a little something today," as he held up the book, "but it isn't going to be steak."

I glared at the gigantic millipede on the front cover of that book and pictured it in ashes. That was it. We were going to burn the book! Burn every one of those horrible bug bodies down to harmless dust. Bud was right. This had to work. We high-fived each other. I gotta tell you, Joel, as amazing as the predicament we were in, even more amazing to me was that Bud was becoming a genius—right before my eyes.

He told me to get Dad's matches out of the worktable drawer and he pulled the cover off of the grill. I had just handed them over when we heard Mom's SUV pull into the driveway. Darn. How were we going to barbecue the buggers with her around? She was already wondering if we were nutzoid. The garage door began to rise.

I whispered to Bud that the only way to do this is later, after she went to help at the church rummage sale this afternoon. Bud said that the only way to insure our safety is for one of us to hold the book shut at all times…Clutching the Bug Encyclopedia to his chest, he ran out the side door and into the house, and I quickly followed.

Later, after I heard the garage open and shut, I went to Bud's room and knocked on his door.

He told me to come in and when I opened the door I saw that he was ready. He was sitting on the edge of his bed in his coat and boots. He had the book in his shaking fingers.

It's show time, I said feeling hopeful. Bud nodded and followed me downstairs into the garage. We didn't talk. He lifted the barbecue hood and tried to put the book inside its black belly. What were we thinking? The book was way too big. Barely a third of it fit inside. We couldn't use the gas grill cause it was out of propane—Dad never kept propane in that tank in winter. I started to cry. Why hadn't we realized it wouldn't fit in there?

Without a word, Bud picked up the book, pulled out several pages, scrunched them in a ball and dropped them in the hibachi. Then he lit a match and dropped it inside on top of the crumpled pages. Almost immediately it snuffed out. Wordlessly, he lit another…and another. We smiled at each other as the pages burst into flames. Finally! We could literally smell victory. Until we saw what happened next, that is. Joel, the bugs (it was the killer bees and mosquito section), frantically flew out from its burning pages…right towards us!

chapter Ten

To: JoelJin@surftwn.comp
From: Elockhardt@wryword.comp *(Continued)*

Bud and I tried to bat away the insects, but it was impossible. There were just so many of them—and more were escaping from the burning pages every second.

"We're gonna die, Em!" Bud screamed, and a giant bee flew right inside his mouth.

Helplessly, I watched him gagging, trying to spit it out, while at the same time, other buzzers tried to get in.

I had my own problems. The bees were in my hair, crawling up my nose, inside my ears. The mosquitos? They were everywhere. Stinging my cheeks, forehead, ears—eyelids. It hurt so bad and I felt the welts rising up.I honestly remember thinking that I didn't want to die like this. NOT LIKE THIS. Then, suddenly (I don't know why), I just knew what to do. I covered the hibachi. Then I ran and opened up the garage door. I ran back, picked up the grill and raced into the backyard. The bees and skeetos that had flown out followed.

I dropped into the snow; face-first and Bud quickly did the same. The bugs were dive-bombing us, but with our winter gear on and the rest of us shielded by snow, we were able to hold them off until they froze to death. Most of them just got so cold; they just sort of dropped around us, their legs and wings jerking grossly as they gave up their lives.

Meanwhile, the bee and skeeto "hotdish" in the hibachi was cooking away. It smelled awful; it was great. Although we'd only gotten rid of a couple pages of bugs, at least we'd conquered some of them. It felt so good.

Bud and I sat there, listening to the sounds of victory until it grew silent. No more bugs pounding away at the cover, trying to escape. But now what?

What were we going to do with the rest of the book? It was too large to burn in our grill and we couldn't even think of trying it on an open fire. A campfire wouldn't work; they would all fly out at once. That would be unimaginable and probably deadly.

Oh—to answer your question, Joel, there is only one name listed as author: Angus (no last name, no date, either.) There is no publisher listed at all. How can that be? Another thing Bud told me: the printing of the text in the book is actually tiny insects—I think it's the ones that you can hardly see alone. But in the book they can move around and change what you're reading. Bud saw it happen before all this started, but he told himself he was seeing things. Yeah, if only that were the truth. Anyway, it was a good idea, Joel. I just wish it had worked. Speaking of which, what are we going to do to get rid of this book forever?

Bud wondered if you had any ideas. So, do you? We're pretty desperate here—and pretty wiped out. I'm so tired, Joel.

Em

Date: March 29, 2005 **Time:** 7:12 p.m. CST.
From: JoelJin@surftwn.comp
To: Elockhardt@wryword.comp
Subject: *Re: Freaked out*

This is bad. Badder than bad but glad you and Bud are okay—and that you got rid of at least some of those things. Skeeters and bees attacking at the same time? I dunno how you guys can stand it. Man, I've been in brain warp all day, trying to come up with a solution. I totally screwed my chemistry experiment. When my beaker on the Bunsen burner boiled over, Mr. Duderwright just about did too—right out of his chair. He accidentally burped while yelling at me. I didn't care. I couldn't even laugh with the rest of the class. I think the kids here are starting to think I'm weird. I'm starting to *feel* weird.

That is dang strange that there is no full author name (Angus...Schmangus?) or publisher listed on the book, but why should we be surprised? With everything that's been going on, it would have been crazy to have something normal connected with that thing. Who would ever admit it? Why would anybody want to do it in the first place? If it was a person. Of course it was a person who wrote it. The bugs couldn't be in control of the whole thing right? Could they? They couldn't have written it themselves...Naw, they couldn't.

Em, I haven't looked at any book the same since all this started. I don't know if I ever will again. I moved the book I got for Christmas about sharks from my bedroom and stuck it under Queen of Mean's bed. I even made sure not to touch the part of the cover that had the Great White's teeth on it. Like my fingers'd get ripped to shreds? Man, I'm losing it. I dunno. I mean you can't be too careful, right? Wrong. What's happening to me?

This is crazy. I'm nowhere near you/that book and I'm going nuts thinking sharks might be after me. I'm more paranoid than normal. I'm wiped out, Em, living with this extreme paranoia.

Sorry for rambling. It doesn't help you. I know that—and helping you is the most important thing.

Okay listen. You need to get that book into something or somewhere where it can't hurt you. Hey, does your Dad still have that old safe sitting out in the shed? Remember, that huge, ugly metal thing that you and I used to play bank robber with and try to crack? He hasn't used it in years, right? You said he trusted the bank deposit boxes much more? Anyway, IF it's still there—is the combination still readable, didn't your Dad write it onto the wallboards once? (Remember how we thought that was so lame and funny, putting your valuables in the safe and then writing the combination on the opposite wall?) Hopefully, the set up is the same. I feel really drained. I need cookies and my stash is dry. Mom made organic carrot bars. That isn't going to cut it. Nothin's going right. IS the safe still there? Huh?

Joel

• •

Date: March 29, 2005 **Time:** 10:08 p.m. CST.
To: JoelJin@surftwn.comp
From: Elockhardt@wryword.comp
Subject: *Re: Freaked out*

Maybe something will go right cause I'm sure the safe is still there—way in the back, partially covered by a tarp. Bud remembers hitting his shin on it last summer when hauling out the gardening tools for Mom. That's a great idea about locking the book up in the safe. REALLY great. That would have to work. Bud agrees—we practically danced around the kitchen when we read it. We're going to get out to the shed and "deposit" those insects once and for all. I'll e-mail you later. See? Even in the midst of this terror and chaos Emily Lockhardt has not lost her sense of puns (nor her shiny blonde hair) and by the way, she LOVES carrot bars. The more organic-y, the better. ;-)

Em

• •

Date: March 29, 2005 **Time:** 11:17 p.m. CST.
To: JoelJin@surftwn.comp
From: Elockhardt@wryword.comp
Subject: *Re: Freaked out*

Joel, we found the safe hiding under about three years of dust and grime—finally got the combination right (time faded the last number and my index finger now has a blister). Anyway, we tossed the book inside and slammed the door shut. Oh my gosh, it's locked away. It feels so awesome! Bud and I feel like we can relax and really breathe for the first time in days. Speaking of which, Bud's already in bed—his asthma was triggered just by being in that musty shed. I am so tired, too. I'm glad those creatures are not in the house.

I gotta tell you; those darn bugs just don't give up, Joel. Ever. While I was fiddling with the lock Bud was holding the book and saw an antenna start to peek out from the middle pages. He held the book closed with all his might but more and more antennas pushed their way to the edge and beyond.

Bud says that it looked like the cockroaches knew what we were up to and were trying to make a getaway.

Figures. Those suckers have been around since the beginning of time, haven't they? I've heard they are becoming immune to poisons and that they could survive a nuclear war. They are so long and black and hairy and gross. Bud said he felt them pushing forward and out and it took all his strength to keep the book from flinging open. Actually, he ended up sitting on the book to keep it shut, but not before one of the ishy things actually made it out. It didn't have long to rejoice, however, because Bud's tennis shoe was on top of it, lickety-split. The crunching sound was both disgusting and enjoyable at the same time. That's how warped we've become in this war with the bugs. That's exactly what if feels like. A war. I'm too young to be a soldier—and far too pretty.

Joel, Bud told me to tell you thanks and that, "you've really turned into a cool dude." I think he's trying to impress you with some sort of California lingo thing.

I'll e-mail you tomorrow. I gotta get up to bed before my legs give out.

Em

• •

Date: March 30, 2005 **Time:** 6:33 a.m. CST.
From: JoelJin@surftwn.comp
To: Elockhardt@wryword.comp
Subject: *Wait a minute! Read THIS!!*

Yo, Em, glad you were finally able to sleep. I mean, you DID SLEEP, didn't you? I mean, you didn't e-mail me in the middle of the night, so I'm hoping that's because you were snoring away. Not that you'd ever snore.

I need to tell you guys that I don't think keeping the book inside the safe will work as a permanent solution. Like, what if your Dad goes out there and decides to open it up, out of the blue? I know it seems unlikely but stranger things have happened, as you and Bud well know.

I think the only way that you guys are really going to be safe is to get rid of the book for good—you will have to kill it and I mean KILL IT. There's no other way. (This is so bizarre; I'm sitting here, telling you to murder a book.)

Just don't feel "too" safe. I would say you and Bud should think of this as a break for a while the bugs are on a weird sort of layaway. Then, you've got to get rid of them for good. I know, I know—but how? I dunno. I'll keep thinking. Later,

Joel

• •

Date: March 30, 2005 **Time:** 5:34 p.m. CST.
To: JoelJin@surftwn.comp
From: Elockhardt@wryword.comp
Subject: *Re: Wait a minute! Read THIS!!*

Too late, Joel. We just got back from the ice show and Bud ran to check the safe. It was open! Dad had been in there getting salt for the driveway and noticed that the safe was all cleaned off.

Dad mumbled something like he could have sworn he had the tarp on that thing and that he thought maybe we'd had a burglar out here.

Ack! Dad can't remember where his glasses are (when he's already wearing them or they're hanging around his neck) and he suddenly remembers there was a tarp on the safe—put there, like three years ago? Give me a break, Joel, come on. It's like the whole world and everything in it is going against us. When I thought about the door being unlocked and opened, I almost screamed, I really did. Once I was able to sort of compose myself I dared ask Dad if he saw anything inside and he said when he reached his hand to feel in the dark, he felt something scurry across his fingers.

He shivered when he told me he figured it was a nest of spiders and that he didn't want anything to do with them, saying that they can have it.

Guess what, Joel? My big, manly dad is afraid of spiders and because of that the book is gone.

Em

chapter Eleven

Date: March 30, 2005 **Time:** 7:17 p.m. CST.
To: Elockhardt@wryword.comp
From: JoelJin@surftwn.comp
Subject: *Re: Wait a minute! Read THIS!!*

Em, I had a strange feeling. You know, it's almost like those bugs "willed" your Dad to open the safe. This is really freaking me out. It's too weird and I don't like it. I know, I know, join the club. I'm sure you understand that you guys are in danger and I don't think you guys should dare go to sleep at the same time. One of you should always keep guard. I also think you should stay together.

So maybe you should sleep the first half of the night, Bud can sit on your floor and read a book or something— sorry, reading a book is probably the last thing he'd wanna do…Anyway, pass the time somehow…and then you guys could switch rooms and you could do the same. Honestly, Em, I really think you both shouldn't sleep at the same time. Cause if you do, that's when they'll make their move. I can feel it. I can really feel it. I know it's late out there so why don't you and Bud figure out who will sleep first and e-mail me in the morning.

Joel

• •

Date: March 31, 2005 **Time:** 5:56 a.m. CST.
To: JoelJin@surftwn.comp
From: Elockhardt@wryword.comp
Subject: *Re: Wait a minute! Read THIS!!*

Bud and I did as you said; except he slept first (he could barely keep his lids up) and I got to sleep about 2:30. I kept thinking I was hearing things—you know—scratches, fluttering, little knocks, etc., but thankfully no bugs emerged. Bud said he kept hearing weird little sounds too, but he also saw nothing. It's almost unbelievable. We're both real tired, but glad to be heading off to school. Yes, Bud's glad to be going to school! Mark this historic day on your calendar.

Joel, thanks for the advice, I don't think we would have thought of it ourselves—we're both getting pretty punchy. (I guess it's 'cause of fear—and of course, lack of sleep). Anyway, I gotta take a shower and get some breakfast. I'm not hungry—neither is Bud. Yes, yet another reason to mark this day. Stupid joke. Anyway, we both know if we don't eat, we'll feel even worse—plus Mom would definitely know something was wrong.

I'll e-mail you later this afternoon. Thanks again, Joel.
Em

• •

Date: March 31, 2005 **Time:** 7:56 a.m. CST.
To: JoelJin@surftwn.comp
From: Elockhardt@wryword.comp
Subject: *Re: Wait a minute! Read THIS!!*

Joel, you're not going to believe this. Mom senses that something is up. She looked at Bud and me real weird this morning, then went into the bathroom and whipped out the ol' thermometer. She said Bud was running a temp of 102!! Mine was actually below normal, so Mom told me I was going to school, but she insisted that Bud stay home! You should have seen the look on his face, Joel. *Complete terror.* It took all the strength I had not to run up and hug him. I don't feel so good, Mom….I lied, rubbing my temples. I have a horrible headache. Wow. A really HORRIBLE aching—in my head. Where in your head? Mom asked. The front part, I said, pointing to my forehead. Mom didn't look overly concerned so I laid it on thicker. Oh, and the side parts really hurt, too—I told her. Both of them. Mom squinted her eyes at me skeptically and said, "Well I'll give you some pain medication then, but you really should attend school—what with that big math test you have today…"

Math? I didn't study for it at all. I'd completely forgotten about that test. And guess what? I DON'T CARE!!!!

Joel, what am I going to do about Bud? How can I leave him here alone with those…*creatures*! Mom's yelling for me to leave for school. Oh Joel, I've got to go. I don't have any choice. It wouldn't be so bad, except for the fact that Mom's going to be gone the whole day at that church rummage sale. Poor Bud. I gotta go. I feel like I'm in another world—dropped inside some crazy video game.

Em

• •

Date: March 31, 2005 **Time:** 9:47 a.m. CST.
From: JoelJin@surftwn.comp
To: Elockhardt@wryword.comp
Subject: *Hey BUD—U there? READ THIS!!!!*

Yo, BUD! I know I'm sending this to Emily, but I don't know your e-mail address, so I can only hope you're reading this. I know the Queen of, ah Janice would be. Listen, dude, I've been thinking about what you're facing. It's a tough predicament but the most important thing is that NO MATTER WHAT…DON'T GO TO SLEEP! I know you're really tired and I realize you're probably sick too (that stinks) but I also know you can be a strong kid sometimes and that you can fight the urge to close your eyes if your life depends upon it. Guess what? I'm pretty dang sure that your life depends on it.

If I were you, I would hole up somewhere in the house dude. Your bedroom, probably. Make sure you check it for the book/bugs first!!! Then, I would shut the heating vents and cram something under the crack in the door. This should keep you safe until Em gets home. But dude, it is not foolproof. Make sure you don't let yourself think so and fall asleep. No sleeping. While the bugs are your number one enemy, sleep is a close second.

You know, now that I think about it, I think you should drink coffee…I know you probably hate it, but you can stand it—add a bunch of sugar. It helps. The caffeine in it will buzz you enough to keep you awake.

Man, I sure hope you're reading this…
Joel

Date: March 31, 2005 **Time:** 10:02 a.m. CST.
To: JoelJin@surftwn.comp
From: Elockhardt@wryword.comp
Subject: *Re: Hey BUD—U there? READ THIS!!!!*

Hey, dude. You know I used to read Em's e-mail from you all the time, but lately I've quit. Musta gotten a conscience or something—Naw, they just weren't very interesting. Anyway, with all that's going on with us here, and all the help you've given us, I just couldn't resist the chance to read the e-mail from you today, glad I did. What ya said makes sense, ha, ha, never thought I'd ever write that to you. I've already drank a cup of black death. Grossamundo. Why do my parents inhale that crap? I must admit tho, I'm feelin wired. I'm going to hole up in my room like you said and try to think of a way out of this mess—Yep I've checked it for the book (probly about 250 times) and seems clear. I won't go to sleep, I can't. I think I'll go get another cup of sugar (with some coffee chucked in) just to be sure…

   Bud

• •

Date: March 31, 2005 **Time:** 11:57 a.m. CST.
From: BuddyBoylockhardt@wryword.comp
To: JoelJin@surftwn.comp
To: Elockhardt@wryword.comp
Subject: *Hey BUD—U there? READ THIS!!!!*

This is crazy. I had to go like a racehorse. I mean, after all that coffee, what'd I expect? I listened hard before I opened that dang bedroom door. Nothing. I made it to the bathroom and was almost back inside my room—I had my hand on the knob when I heard them clunking up the stairs. Loud, dude, really loud. Man, they were there so fast. I ran past them and downstairs. Weird. I haven't heard nothing since. I hid in the broom closet for at least an hour. This is the first time I've snuck out of there—to let you know—in case something happens to me. I don't know what to do. Do I try and go back upstairs? Where are they and why didn't they follow me down here? What are they doing? Are they trying to torture me?

Joel I know you're at school, but after you see this if you got any more ideas, tell me...Wait a minute...I hear something. I don't like this. Oh man I hear 'em comin'.

chapter Twelve

Date: March 31, 2005 **Time:** 4:12 p.m. CST.
To: JoelJin@surftwn.comp
From: Elockhardt@wryword.comp
Subject: *Where's Bud?!!*

He's gone, Joel. Bud's gone! When I got home from school I found the patio door open and Bud was nowhere to be found. I would have been home sooner but Ms. Weinster asked me to stay after school so "we could talk" I told her, thank you for the offer, but I couldn't. She told me it wasn't an offer and that I not only "could" stay after, but I would—or else. I couldn't believe that she was making me stay after on the day Bud needs me most. And all because she's worried about me. She wanted me to explain why I failed the math test today. I just sat there. What was I supposed to say? I failed because I didn't study, because insects from the bug book are terrorizing my brother and me? I failed because I'm afraid that my life is in danger and all because of bugs? I failed and it's all Mrs. Robbins fault? Even though it IS, sure, she would have believed that…NOT!

On the other hand maybe I should have told her I was worried about my brother—worried that those vicious creatures would harm Bud—or worse? Right. I'm losing my mind, Joel. I'm losing what's left to lose, anyway. BUD is GONE!!!! Joel, he's GONE! How? Where? I don't know what to do. I don't know where to look this time. Mom will be back within the hour—what am I going to tell her? What can I tell her? I don't know where he is, but I know who took him. You're darn right I know who/what took him. Joel, this is too much. TOO MUCH! I feel like I'm in a fog that never clears up. Oh dear. Oh dear Lord, is Bud okay? IS HE? Or is he…could he already be…you don't think that he's, you don't—do you? DO YOU???

I read his e-mail to us but it offers no clue. Is he cold? Is he suffering? Joel, the keyboard is all wet, and I didn't think I had any tears left…You ARE coming tomorrow, right? That's the only thing that's keeping me going.

Joel…are you home yet? Are you there? Oh, how I pray that you're there. Help me, Joel. Tell me what to do!

Em

• •

Date: March 31 **Time:** 3:23 p.m. CST.
From: JoelJin@surftwn.comp
To: Elockhardt@wryword.comp
Subject: *Re: Where's Bud?!!*

Man, this stinks! I'm sorry. I can't believe it's really happening. I feel so far away, but I also feel so close—I can smell your fear. I swear. We're all coming, just like planned.

Listen Em. You gotta pull it together…for Bud's sake. You gotta look for Bud—right away. Get off the web and check everywhere outside. See if you can find any pieces of clothing he might have dropped, see if you can see any trails in the snow. The longer you wait, the harder it will be. They took him somewhere, we know that, but where?

I know you're tired and scared and ready to curl up in a ball under your covers and never come back out, but you can't dangit! Bud needs you. And whether you like it or not, you're the only person who can help him now.

This probably is stupid, but did you check the garage roof again? I'm sure you did but if you didn't, do it.

Get moving now. You're going to e-mail me back that you got this message, then you're going to put your coat and boots back on and go outside and search for any sign of Bud.

Joel

• •

Date: March 31, 2005 **Time:** 4:46 p.m. CST.
To: JoelJin@surftwn.comp
From: Elockhardt@wryword.comp
Subject: *Re: Where's Bud?!!*

Yes Joel, I got your message. I know I have to go looking for Bud, but I'm afraid of what I might find. But...I know I have to go and I know I have to go now...

Em

• •

Date: March 31, 2005 **Time:** 6:12 p.m. CST.
To: JoelJin@surftwn.comp
From: Elockhardt@wryword.comp
Subject: *Re: Where's Bud?!!*

Bud's still missing...but I did find the book. It was back in the garage, but this time it was way back in the corner under some old tires. Joel, as I reached down and pulled off the last tire, the book was there. I saw that it was open to the tarantula page—but there were no tarantulas there. It was blank, except for the word *tarantula*, which I now know was being spelled out by other bugs…this is crazy.

Joel, I heard the neighbor's motorcycle rev up and I ran to make sure George wasn't stopping by to offer Bud a ride. He wasn't, thank goodness. But when I got back to the book, the tarantulas were back on their page. Their blackness, little beady eyes, legs, legs and *more* hairy legs. Then the book snapped shut right before my eyes. I opened it back up to the tarantula page and they were gone. The page was blank. I can't believe any of this. Where were they when they weren't in the book? Does this have anything to do with where Bud is?

I've searched everywhere on our property and I haven't seen a trace of him. Mom and Dad will be home any minute. I've put the book back in the safe for the time being…do you think that's okay? What do I tell the folks about Bud, Joel? What can I possibly say? I need more time to search for Bud. Help me.

Em

• •

Date: March 31, 2005 **Time:** 6:52 p.m. CST.
From: JoelJin@surftwn.comp
To: Elockhardt@wryword.comp
Subject: *Re: Where's Bud?!!*

Yo, Em good job finding the book, and yeah! you should definitely put it back in the safe for now. I'll be there tomorrow afternoon.

What to tell your folks? You have to act dumb. Tell them Bud was already gone when you got home (which is true) and that you figure he probably took off with one of his buddies (which is possible—even though we know it isn't what happened).

It should buy you some time with your folks. I mean, it's not like Bud hasn't pulled stuff like this before, right? Remember last spring, when he and that Mike Jansen dude skipped school and went to the movie theater for the entire day...*and night*? And what about the time he up and decided to play Huck Finn and try out his homemade raft on a trek down the Mississippi? If he hadn't been such an expert swimmer, he'd probably been a goner. What a dope. Your folks finally heard from him the next morning, remember? Bud was too afraid to let them know what he'd done and he'd ended up camping by the river that night. That raft thing seemed to get to him like maybe he learned something and now this and it isn't even his fault—this time.

Joel

• •

Date: March 31, 2005 **Time:** 8:15 p.m. CST.
To: JoelJin@surftwn.comp
From: Elockhardt@wryword.comp
Subject: *Re: Where's Bud?!!*

That'll work. I can still see Bud's face as he told my outraged parents, that the reason they stayed so late was because it was a multiplex theater. They had to catch each and every movie...right?

What a dope is right. I remember laughing so hard...Oh, and the river "cruise" he took, is legendary now in my family.

All of our aunts and uncles use Bud's bad example to scare our cousins into behaving and grandpa brings it up almost every time he sees him.

Oh, Joel, I'm so worried about Bud, I can't stand it. I now truly know what excruciating really feels like. I thought I knew what it felt like. I thought it was excruciating when John Farkas not only didn't ask me to the teen dance at the fire hall, but actually asked my arch-nemesis—the over-made-up, under-intelligent Sherina Sastrub—instead. But that's not excruciating at all. This is. This is the real deal, and I hate it.

Em

• •

Date: March 31, 2005 **Time:** 9:58 p.m. CST.
To: JoelJin@surftwn.comp
From: Elockhardt@wryword.comp
Subject: *Re: Where's Bud?!!*

He's still gone. My folks are ready to murder him—Dad just got back from checking the movie theaters, and they've just about called everybody Bud ever grinned at to see if they've heard from him or seen him. They know he'd never try the river thing again—certainly not in winter at least, but I know a lot of scary things are running through their minds.

Everything is really bizarre, Joel. Mom keeps hugging me and Dad is constantly pacing around. When he looks at me, it's like I'm not there. His mind is searching for Bud. Wondering where Bud could be. Willing himself to figure out how to find Bud. Mom made boxed mac and cheese for supper and nobody ate. I tried, but I couldn't. They didn't even try and make me. Without Bud here, it was so quiet, our forks tapping against the plates sounded like kettledrums...it was creepy.

I've gone over our yard at least five times, and still I see no clue—nothing. The weather is warming up and the snow is almost gone now, so that doesn't help find tracks either.

Dad's glasses are all smudged; I don't think he can see much but he doesn't seem to care. He looks older somehow. His jaw is clenched, his face is all white and I haven't seen his smile for so long. He's the one who always finds the humor in everything—him and Bud, but not this time for either of them. The neighbor, Mrs. Sentilian, brought over a chocolate cake, but we haven't touched it. If I even think about eating it, my throat feels like it's closing. Joel, Mom looks so little, sitting curled up in the recliner in the family room. She's always been petite but how come I never noticed how small she really is until now? She seems almost like a child. Her long brown hair is sort of back in a ponytail, but parts of it are coming loose and she doesn't have any makeup on. She's so pale, Joel. Like she is made of glass and like she could break if she has one more thing happen to worry her. She's scared. Dad's scared. I'm petrified.

Bud! Where are you? Oh, Joel, I think I have to tell my folks about the Bug Book, and all that's been happening! I know they won't (can't) believe it, and I know the bugs won't do anything while Mom and Dad are around, but still, at least I'd know I was telling them the truth. I can't take this anymore. If I didn't have you to tell this nightmare to, I'd be crazy by now. More. Come to think of it...maybe I already am. Am I crazy Joel? Am I? I think I might be. I really do.

Em

Date: March 31, 2005 **Time:** 10:38 p.m. CST.
From: JoelJin@surftwn.comp
To: Elockhardt@wryword.comp
Subject: *Re: Where's Bud?!!*

No, you're not crazy, Em. What's happening to you guys is crazy—but you aren't—and neither is Bud. More than usual I mean. There's nothing else you can do tonight—it's dark now. I'll be there tomorrow afternoon and we'll come up with a plan. Say your prayers like always, only MORE (I will even try and say some too), and try to sleep. I know you won't be able to sleep, but at least rest—because there's one thing I can tell you for sure, Em—you're going need it. See ya tomorrow.

Joel

• •

Date: March 31, 2005 **Time:** 11:57 p.m. CST.
To: JoelJin@surftwn.comp
From: Elockhardt@wryword.comp
Subject: *Re: Where's Bud?!!*

I went out back to make sure the safe is still locked and it was, but Joel, as I was heading back up, I swear I heard the muffled sound of somebody calling my name...and Joel, it sounded just like...Bud!!!

chapter Thirteen

To: JoelJin@surftwn.comp
From: Elockhardt@wryword.comp *(Continued)*

I raced right back to the safe and put my ear to the door, but I didn't hear anything. I must have sat there like that for ten minutes. If Mom or Dad had seen me sitting there—my ear glued to that old safe, listening for Bud's voice? What would they think? Oh Joel, I guess it must have been my imagination. But I swear, it sounded so much like him...like he was trapped in that safe. I wonder if I'm losing my mind. Do you wonder if I'm losing my mind? If I am...will it ever come back...and if this were real, would I want it to?

I gotta go. Mom and Dad want to talk to me—they're really worried about Bud—join the club...I don't know how long I can pretend I don't know anything, even though I really don't know anything for sure. You know what I mean?

Joel, please let me know if you think of anything I can do to find Bud and get rid of those bugs—ANYTHING—no matter how weird it might seem to be. Bring your laptop on the plane.

Em

• •

Date: April 1, 2005 **Time:** 5:33 a.m. CST.
From: JoelJin@surftwn.comp
To: Elockhardt@wryword.comp
Subject: *Whassup with Bud?*

Em, I'll see ya soon, but I know you'll e-mail me any minute now to tell me that you found Bud.

I've been trying all night to figure out what your next step should be and I haven't come up with much. Ok nothing. My gut tells me Bud is somewhere close. I dunno. I just think he isn't far away. I guess it's cause we figure the bugs nabbed him in the kitchen, and seems like they never stray too far. But they've never had the chance to stray too far before...until now.

What matters most now is that you've got the bug book. They seem to need that thing. I mean they always go back to it when they're done with whatever they do, don't they? I think the answer is crammed within its pages, Em. Those awful things hold the key. Maybe there's a clue about Bud in the book.

When I get there I will take the book and look, page by page, for some sort of clue. I might be able to spot something. Dangit Em, I probably won't come up with anything—but at least I'll be doing something, right? Dad's calling—gotta go. One more thing, don't you dare try this yourself. It won't be safe. I'll do it when I get there. I mean it.

Joel

• •

Date: April 1, 2005 **Time:** 7:56 a.m. CST.
To: JoelJin@surftwn.comp
From: Elockhardt@wryword.comp
Subject: *Re: Whassup with Bud?*

Bud's still missing. My folks have been up all night. They made me go to bed, but of course I just lay there, worrying.

Joel, they've already called the police. They came out last night and interviewed us. They said they couldn't even begin to look for him until he's been missing for over 24 hours. My folks of course had to tell them about the time Bud was gone so long at the movie theater, and the raft thing, so the cops are pretty sure he's just "goofing off" somewhere.

Oh, I wish it were true. I can tell that even Mom and Dad don't think he's off having a good time, you know, because he's been gone so long and he was running a fever and stuff…and like you said, that river thing really seemed to straighten him up. He's grown up so much in the last year-and-a-half. We've all noticed it.

The whole thing with the police was so bizarre. The cops act just like they do on TV.

They pull out their note pads, asking questions, then furiously scribbling down our answers. I did like you told me to do and told them he was gone when I got home and that I had no idea where he would've gone—which unfortunately, is the truth.

We had a guy cop and a woman cop. The woman was older, kind of reminded me of Mrs. Robbins. She had gray in her hair (that was pulled back in a tight bun thing) and thin lips that never smiled. Her eyes were all squinty and you could tell by her snide little comments that she thought Bud was a troublemaker and that my folks were wasting her time. It made me mad. The guy was younger, barely looked much older than Bud. He seemed to care at least. He kept smiling and telling us that boys will be boys and 16 year olds run off sometimes but everything should turn out just fine.

Since they left Mom's been crying almost continuously and Dad's eyes look all red and gummy.

This is getting way too serious and way too frightening. We're all just kind of sitting here like statues—when they aren't driving around the neighborhood, searching, and searching again. Nobody can eat. It's awful. AWFUL.

Before I'd read your e-mail, I already decided I needed to scour that book—I can think of no other place to turn for answers. I can't wait for you to get here. I've gotta do it. He's my brother and I can't just sit here, hearing the clock tick and worrying so much I feel like I've got stomach flu. Mom and Dad are just sitting there in the living room—no TV, no radio, they're just sitting there, staring at…nothing. It's bizarre and wrong. I'm going out to the shed and look through the book now. Wish me luck; pray for me; cross your fingers. Joel, I mean it…I can tell…I'm going to need it. GET HERE NOW. Did I mention pray for me and Bud? Well—do it!

Em

• •

Date: April 1, 2005 **Time:** 9:59 a.m. CST.
To: JoelJin@surftwn.comp
From: Elockhardt@wryword.comp
Subject: *Re: Whassup with Bud?*

Joel, when I opened the safe and reached my right hand inside for the book, I was immediately stung by wasps! I don't know how many actually got me, but my hand has swollen up to twice its normal size. I managed to grab onto the book anyway, but the venom from the stings seemed to paralyze it, and the book slipped from my numb fingers.

Quickly I whipped my hand back out and slammed the safe door. But six of the wasps were still stinging my hand and they ended up outside the safe, away from the book, with me. As soon as that door shut, they left my body and careened their bodies into the door—they were so desperate, to get back inside Joel. Over and over, they smashed their wings and heads, until each and every one of them literally squashed themselves to death.

I must admit, and it scares me to do so, that I enjoyed watching them kill themselves. What does this mean for my soul? I can't believe how angry I am. Look what they're doing to me. What am I turning into? How am I possibly going to look for Bud, if those bugs keep stopping me from getting hold of their book? I think they know my plans, Joel. Seriously, it's like they're reading my mind.

Mom just walked in here to get some more coffee, I think, but she's just standing there, holding her empty cup, staring at the coffee pot. Staring and not moving. I said her name and Joel, guess what? As soon as she glanced at me my right hand un-swelled—just like somebody'd let the air out of it.

That's just what I needed. I am going to pour Mom some coffee and walk her back into the living room, then I will return to the shed—and no matter what those bugs have in store for me, I'm going to get a hold of that book.

Em

chapter Fourteen

Date: April 1, 2005 **Time:** 10: 31 a.m. CST.
From: JoelJin@surftwn.comp
To: Elockhardt@wryword.comp
Subject: *Re: Whassup with Bud?*

Em, stop. Don't mess with the book. If they got Bud they can get you, too. It's too dangerous. Wait'll I get there. We'll think up some other way to look for Bud. Or I'll at least have a better chance of fighting them off. Promise me, Em. I can feel you're in danger—real danger, Em. E-mail me back right now and promise you'll stay away from that freakin' book!
Joel

• •

Date: April 1, 2005 **Time:** 10:34 a.m. CST.
From: JoelJin@surftwn.comp
To: Elockhardt@wryword.comp
Subject: *WHERE R U?!*

Em! Why aren't you answering me? It's WAY TOO DANGEROUS!! EM, E-MAIL ME IMMEDIATELY!!! IMMEDIATELY!!! I'm REALLY ticked off! Big time!
Joel

• •

Date: April 1, 2005 **Time:** 10:57 a.m. CST.
From: JoelJin@surftwn.comp
To: Elockhardt@wryword.comp
Subject: *Re: WHERE R U?!*

I hope you're in the bathroom or something. I mean you better be. I'm jumpin out of my skin!
Joel

• •

Date: April 1, 2005 **Time:** 11:27 a.m. CST.
To: JoelJin@surftwn.comp
From: Elockhardt@wryword.comp
Subject: *Re: WHERE R U?!*

I don't know where to start! I've been in the shed all this time (I guess Mom and Dad must've dozed off in the living room) and you'll never believe in a trillion years what I've found.

I was determined to look inside that book to see if I could find any clue about Bud…and what a clue I found Joel.

I opened the safe and once again reached inside—fully expecting my hand to be assaulted by wasps or something—but amazingly enough I was able to pull out the book, drop next to the safe, my elbow resting inside (ready to pop the sucker back in if need be), and open it up.

Pages and pages of all sorts of insects and bugs. Kinds I've never ever heard of—and never want to again. One page had a huge picture of one beetle blown up so big you could see its nose hairs, another showed a photo of thousands of mosquitos wingin' around above some slew.

Joel, I was shaking so badly that when I would think I'd see the bugs squirm or hop, I wasn't sure if it was me causing it or them. The pages seemed to quiver from them though; I think they were trying to scare me (it worked), but for some reason couldn't quite make it off the page this time.

So there I sat, on that cold dirt floor, my butt growing numb, staring at page after page of bug after bug and I was almost through the first half when I saw it: a red bandana. It was hanging from some shrub in a jungle—Brazil, of all places. (At least that's what the bugs spelled out.)

Okay Joel, now here is where it gets crazy. I just realized how crazy that last line was. It's all crazy. You know that Bud's been known to wear a bandana…and it struck me as odd that an ol' faded bandana would be hangin' off some shrub in South America…right in the middle of the picture of these weird dung beetles.

I searched that page so closely that I literally went cross-eyed. Nothing more…there.

When I turned to the next page, I was treated to a blown up silverfish, grinning at me. I literally jumped back a bit—it was that ugly. I was about to flip the page when I saw it. It was almost completely covered by this bug. Still, I wasn't sure. So I got up and searched through the storage boxes until I'd found the magnifying glass Mom'd used when we'd had lice, and I ran back to the safe. Tilting my head to the side to allow the most light of the dim wattage to reach the pages, I held up the magnifying glass over that part. My heart thumped into my throat, my stomach flipped over and I began to cry.

It was a slipper. A blue slipper. And Joel, it had a hole where the big toe went. Joel, it was Bud's slipper. It was. There was no denying it!

Yet again I wondered: am I completely mad? How was all of this possible? How did Bud's slipper get to Brazil? Even after all I'd been through, I was having a difficult time believing I was seeing what I was seeing. How did those bugs manage to get Bud's stuff inside their book? HOW? And where was MY BROTHER?

I turned to the next page, magnifying glass ready, and looked over every inch. Nothing. I turned the page yet again…nothing. Again and again and again. Nothing! No more of Bud's clothing, no sign of anything at all. Nothing but disgusting bugs that is.

Wait. Somebody's in the driveway. Hang on. Grandma and Grandpa just got here. Everybody is so worried about Bud. They're all crying—even Grandpa. They are yelling for me to come.

Em

• •

Date: April 1, 2005 **Time:** 11:59 a.m. CST.
To: JoelJin@surftwn.comp
From: Elockhardt@wryword.comp
Subject: *Re: WHERE R U?!*

Grandma and Grandpa are so sad and freaked out, Joel. It just seems to make this feel all the more real and scary. Grandma's holding on to two kerchiefs instead of her usual one, and she keeps mopping below her eyes and nose. She's wearing that black velour pantsuit that she wears to church and her cheeks are all red. I think she has probably hugged me about 25 times since they've been here. Normally that would be annoying but she seems softer today and she smells like cinnamon toast. Her hugs make me feel safe for at least the time I'm in them. Grandpa's kind of hovering between angry and sad. One minute he's grabbing one of Grandma's kerchiefs to wipe his tears and the next he's yelling at Bud for worrying us—even though he knows Bud's not here to hear it. Gramps just pulled on his galoshes and down coat. He says he's going to scour the forest preserve to find his Buddy. He thinks Bud's out in the middle of those woods somewhere. Mom, Dad and Grandma have told him he can't go traipsing out back; he'd end up sick, hurt or lost himself. Whoa. I'd better not write what Gramps said back. He's got a mouth on him sometimes, but I have to admit I feel the same way. He just wants to do something to help find Bud. Me too. The folks told him he'd be much better off driving around the neighborhood to look for Bud and he finally agreed. I can tell he knows he won't find Bud that way though. It's like he senses something. That Bud is not somewhere easily found. He's so right. How did everything go so wrong?

Finally I've got a chance to go back outside and open the safe again. Grandma made Mom lie down and Grandpa and Dad—armed with cell phones are driving around searching for any sign of Bud. Grandpa's heading east; Dad's heading west, or vice-versa. I don't know. I don't think it really matters. Do you? I'll let you know if I find anything…

Em

• •

Date: April 1, 2005 **Time:** 12:53 p.m. CST.
To: JoelJin@surftwn.comp
From: Elockhardt@wryword.comp
Subject: *Re: WHERE R U?!*

Joel, I don't know how to tell you this. Actually, I'm not sure I'm even right about it all. All I know is that after spending over an hour paging through that horrible thing, I spotted something…I mean…someone.

It's on the page with something called "ambush" bugs and I see a person way back in the distance, under some huge tree, but his back is turned in the picture, so of course, I can't be sure.

But the truth is, he is wearing what looks like a white sweatshirt with some red writing on the back and blue jeans.

I know this is crazy, I really do, but I feel in my gut that the picture of the guy in that picture is…Bud. Joel, Bud has a sweatshirt just like that, and he lives in his jeans. No, I'm not positive it's him—it could be anybody—but I have a feeling that it's Bud, and Joel, I'm sure you understand what I have to do now. I'm sure you understand that I have no choice. I'm not sure how I'll accomplish it, but I know that somehow I'm going to have to get inside that book myself, in order to get Bud out!

Joel, quickly, I just want you to know that even though I always knew we were best friends, you have proven to me, without a doubt, that you are truly the best of the best.

If, for some reason, I should "disappear" just like Bud, and we aren't able to come back—don't come after us. If *we* can't get out then you wouldn't be able to, either. It makes no sense to do it. Just make sure that the book is destroyed. Yes, I know what that would mean. But Joel, you'd have no choice. You can't allow you or any other kids to be tortured and/or killed too! I know Bud would agree…

I must go to the book now. I love ya. Wish me luck, and for crying out loud, never forget: The EmJo's!

Em

• •

Date: April 1, 2005 **Time:** 1:21 a.m. CST.
From: JoelJin@surftwn.comp
To: Elockhardt@wryword.comp
Subject: *Re: WHERE R U?!*

EM, NOOOOOOOOOO!!!! DON'T GO BACK OUT THERE!!!! PLEASE!!!!! We'll be there in less than 12 hours! WAIT FOR ME BEFORE YOU OPEN THAT SAFE, EM!!!! WAIT!!!
Joel

• •

Date: April 1, 2005 **Time:** 1:33 p.m. CST.
To: JoelJin@surftwn.comp
From: Elockhardt@wryword.comp
Subject: *Re: WHERE R U?!*

I can't wait, Joel—you know that. Bud is in danger, and he needs me...now! I have to get his inhaler to him—what if he can't breathe? He doesn't have much time, Joel—I can feel it. I know he needs me and by the way? If I do end up saving him, it will be awesome to remind him of that over and over every day for the rest of our lives. ;-) I'm out of here...
Em

chapter Fifteen

Date: April 1, 2005 **Time:** 2:30 p.m. CST.
From: JoelJin@surftwn.comp
To: Elockhardt@wryword.comp
Subject: *Re: WHERE R U?!*

Em, why haven't you e-mailed me yet? Where are you? Are you,dang it, I don't wanna think about it.

Our flight was delayed but we should be there by 6:00 tonight. Believe it or not, Janice seems worried about Bud. I guess she's not as bad as all that. Or maybe she is. I dunno what to think. She came to me last night and told me she's read some of my e-mails to you—once when I got up to go to the bathroom and another time when Mom was rearranging the living room. I had to help Dad move the couch.

She said she thought we were making up some stupid story together! She laughed about it then, but that now she admitted she kind of believes it might be true and she sorta believes us. Hard to believe, isn't it? She made me promise I'd tell her what's going on…I dunno, maybe. I think I will need to talk to somebody about this.

What will I find when we get to Minnesota, Em? Are you going to be there…is Bud?

If you're missing like Bud then I'm going after you, whatever the heck that means. I don't have any idea how, but I won't quit until I find the two of you.

Em, I'm hoping that you found Bud and everything's okay, and you're just sleeping right now.

Ma just got off of her cell phone. She's crying. She told me that your mother just called and that you're missing now, too! This is a day nightmare. I can't believe any of this is happening. I don't know why I'm talking to you like you're there reading this—but I can't help it. I can't swallow real well right now. This stinks. Gotta go

Joel

• •

Date: April 1, 2005 **Time:** 7:34 p.m. CST.
From: JoelJin@surftwn.comp
To: JaniceJin@surftwn.comp
Subject: *What's the dang hold up?*

Dang it, Janice, when are you and Dad going to get us checked in at the hotel and get over here? Em and Bud are still missing and the cops are in the other room with the Lockhardts right now. It stinks! Everybody's hugging and crying. Ma is trying real hard not to—she wants to support Mrs. Lockhardt.

So far, I haven't even been able to get into the shed—let alone check the safe for the book. I think I will have to wait until later—when people fall asleep—or at least until they zone out more…

I hope that once I find them, I'll be able to bring them back. What's weird, is that part of me wants to grab you, Ma and Dad and get back on the plane and head home. I want to forget everything of the past week. I'm really scared. I know I have to help Em and Bud—except I really have no idea how I'm supposed to do it. Not a good plan.

Joel

• •

Date: April 1, 2005 **Time:** 7:59 p.m. CST.
From: JoelJin@surftwn.comp
To: JaniceJin@surftwn.comp
Subject: *You won't believe this*

Im shakkkingsobad. I can harrdly type thisss. Hang on. I gotta settle down a sec…breathe deep. Heart is pounding so loud.Ok. I told them all I needed to think and went out into the shed. I couldnt find the light that place was dark and wet. I felt the string from the ceiling bulb hit my cheek and I jumped so high, my head hit the ceiling. I pulled the string and saw the safe. It was open but just a little and there was this stink. STINK. I leaned over the safe and smelled something I'd never smelled before—don't ever wanna smell again. I opened the door to the safe cuz I had to. Why aren't you and Dad here yet??

The stink that ripped over me was indescribable. I covered my mouth and my eyes. My stomach was churning but that wasn't the worst part. The worst part was the bugs that crawled out of the safe. Into the shed. On me. I guess they were biting me, but it was their smell that freaked me out most.

I couldn't breathe. I pushed them off of me and they crawled back on. They must be stinkbugs. *Oh, the smell!* It was sorta like the smell when you and I found that wormy coon in the back yard—only worse. My stomach hurt and I

94

threw up. I think that's what saved me. They took off crawling back into the safe and the book. Never thought barfing would be so helpful. Glad they hated it. Then I sat down right in my own mess beside the safe, reached into its shadows expecting to find bug book, but—gross my fingers were drenched in something wet and slippery. I'm not saying this to rude you out Janice (okay I kinda am), but it felt like boogers. A whole bunch of gooey greasy boogers. Jerking my hand back out and seeing the greenish gray gunk clinging to it, that's what it looked like. *Boogers.* But I knew, I don't know how, I just knew it was slime. Slime from them.

I dragged my hand across the top of my jeans and reached back in. After smelling their putrid stink, slime wasn't about to stop me—no dang way. I reached into the gross glob that surrounded the book and pulled til it was in my hand. It was slippery; it flew through my fingers, hitting the mower dropping to the floor slime trailing from the wall after it.

Picking up the book I sat under the light bulb down there and opened it up. Every kind of bug insect and spider you could ever imagine (some you never could), stared out of those glossy pages. Em was right. This was one of the most imppresive books I had ever seen or held. I was pretty gooey by now, the slime on both my hands, my jeans, and even in my hair...I didn't care. I kept turning pages searching for Bud and Em. I found the page Em had talked 'bout seein' Bud—and it was just like she'd described cept there wasn't a boy under the big tree.

Where did Bud go? Was he eaten by the insides of this horrad book? Where was Em? I kept turning. If it hadn't have been for the little quiver of the paper, I never would have seen them at the bottom of page 100 and something. I brought the book a fraction away from my eyes. There, huddled on a grassy hill, I saw a boy and a girl surrounded by zillions of bright red lady bugs! Everybody says how benign they are. Ha! You know how bad their bites hurt?

It was Em and Bud. Their mouths were opened wide…I could tell that they were screaming! I can't take this. I can't!
joel

chapter Sixteen

Date: April 1, 2005 **Time:** 8:16 p.m. CST.
To: JoelJin@surftwn.comp
From: JaniceJin@surftwn.comp
Subject: *Re: You won't believe this*

JJ, you're right. Like, seriously, you can't do this. The fear in your email made my arm hairs go up. I've been thinking about all of this and I've decided that YOU CAN'T GO BACK OUT THERE. Think about it. It makes no sense for you to go get trapped in that book with them—and maybe eaten alive too. Like what good would that do Emily and Bud? You know Em would feel terrible if she knew she caused your death. Dad and I stopped by Grandma and Grandpa's house and they just won't let us leave. You know how upset they were that we are staying in a hotel instead of with them. But when Dad explained that a one-bedroom condo would be a bit small for six people, they kind of understood. I told Dad we should get to the Lockhardt's but he said he talked to Mom and that there are just too many people in the house now as it is. We're coming by later tonight. I don't know what to do.

You've got to tell Mom right now. She'll believe you. I really think she will. Especially if you show her the picture you just wrote about—the picture in the book of Emily and her brother. How can she not believe you?

Tell her. I know you're going to be mad at me for this... but, like if you don't tell her? Then I will when Dad and I get there tonight. I'm sorry, I know that will make you mad, but I'm not ready to attend your funeral...yet.

E-mail me right back and don't try to lie to me, because I'll find out and tell anyway.

Janice

• •

Date: April 1, 2005 **Time:** 8:22 p.m. CST.
To: JaniceJin@surftwn.comp
From: JoelJin@surftwn.comp
Subject: *Re: You won't believe this*

Don't you dare JJ me.I hate you. How can you threaten me? I trusted you! How stupid. I won't forgive you for this, Queen of Mean—never!

I will show Ma the book—but only because you're making me do it! I'm telling you that I know there's nothing adults can do to get them out—I can feel it! For some reason the bugs in the book only respond to kids.

I just can't believe you're making me do this—and remember: I WILL NEVER FORGET IT!

Joel

• •

Date: April 1, 2005 **Time:** 8:49 p.m. CST.
To: JaniceJin@surftwn.comp
From: JoelJin@surftwn.comp
Subject: *Re: You won't believe this*

There. I told her! Are you happy? Are you happy? Good. Cause nobody else is. I went and got her off the couch and told her I had to show her something out back. She didn't complain or even say much, cause Mrs. Lockhardt was sleeping on the chair in the corner. She just followed me.

I led her outside to the shed right to the safe. Just like I figured, there were no bugs cause an adult was right there. I opened the book and looked 'til I reached the page I'd seen them on. I told her there was something in the book that she had to see. I told her to sit...and I grabbed a crate and turned it upside down.

I said, "Ma, I am scared about Bud and Em" and handed her the book and she looked for a sec then looked back at me. She asked me what the silly book has to do with Bud and Em. Her eyes were all wet. I pointed where I'd seen them. "What, Joel? What's so important about a pile of leaves?" She asked, blowing her nose. She wanted to know what does that have to do with the kids. I grabbed the book back and looked and looked and looked. There was nothing but that bare hill. Bud and Em were gone. I started saying how I thought I'd seen them in the book and Ma looked worried. She patted my head, kissed me and then lead me back inside.

Janice, are you happy now? Bud and Em are gone and Ma thinks I'm nuts. Thanks. I'll tell you something. I am going right back out there and get that book and search until I find them—that is if it's not too late. I'm going to get them out of there—even if it means I have to go in there to do it. And Janice, you can't stop me so don't try!

Joel
Ps. I hate you

• •

Date: April 1, 2005 **Time:** 9:16 p.m. CST.
To: JoelJin@surftwn.comp
From: JaniceJin@surftwn.comp
Subject: *Re: You won't believe this*

Like I know exactly how you feel. I hate you too. Dad and I are on our way. Don't move! You're not going to listen to me, are you? At the very least, bring a weapon of some sort and maybe even bug killer! I'm sure you can find some in the shed or their basement. Listen, I only said all that because I don't want you hurt—Mom and Dad would be crushed and I don't want to be an only child, yet, so please, PLEASE be prepared and be careful. Better yet—wait for me to get there. Sorry that I made you do that. Okay?
Janice

• •

Date: April 1, 2005 **Time:** 9: 23 p.m. CST.
From: JoelJin@surftwn.comp
To: JaniceJin@surftwn.comp
Subject: *Re: You won't believe this*

No way am I waiting. Great idea about weapons and bug killer. I'll do it.

I think I've figured out how to get into the book. Instead of me going to them, I have to let them come and get me. I will sit out there by the safe and wait. It's just a matter of time until they realize a kid is there and then they will come and get me.

I don't know what kind of bugs it'll be this time, and that kinda scares me, yet still, I think I've got a good shot at being kidnapped into the book, just like Bud and Em were.

If we all get through this okay I don't wanna see another bug again as long as I'm alive. *Is* there a country anywhere that doesn't have any bugs? If there is that'd be so sweet. That'd be the place for me.

Take care of the folks.Help them get through this. Janice, one more thing, even though I still kinda hate you if I don't, come back, you can have my MP3 player. (I know you've been going into my room when I'm gone and using it anyway.)

Joel

P.s. I sorta forgive you for now

chapter Seventeen

Date: April 1, 2005 **Time:** 10:56 p.m. CST.
To: JoelJin@surftwn.comp
From: JaniceJin@surftwn.comp
Subject: *What is going on?!*

I've been sitting here, in the downstairs bathroom at the Lockhardt's in front of this computer, waiting to hear from you. I guess you haven't sorta forgiven me, 'cause you wouldn't keep me wondering like this if you had.

You OWE me! They all think I have some sort of stomach crisis. Emily's grandmother has knocked on the door twice already. The first time she wondered if I needed a coupla spoonfuls of that pink stuff. Like gross! I told her no, I do NOT have THAT kind of problem and she said something like, it's nothing to be embarrassed about and shuffled off. Bout fifteen minutes later she knocked and started whispering through the door about the wonders of dried plums and how very important it is to maintain a high fiber diet. She was standing there outside the door with a bowl of prunes for me, Joel, while I'm in the bathroom! Like gross and grosser still! Like as if THAT isn't strange enough, I can't believe for a moment that you are trapped in that book.

I just can't. Joel, if you ever cared about me—I mean the folks—please e-mail me now and let me know that you're okay. Wait a minute, I mean if you ever didn't hate me for a while then let me know that Bud and Emily are okay, too. Tell me that you're messing with me. All three of you, messing with the Queen of Mean. It'd actually be kind of funny. What if I admit I deserve it? Tell me. Otherwise this is positively insane. This is positively insane.

How come you couldn't get back out? You took the weapons I mentioned, didn't you? Like what's the problem? What am I saying? You're not even there to read this. And I'm supposed to believe that you're trapped inside some crazy book, surrounded by ferocious bugs? Right. This is too much. TOO MUCH.

I see that I'm writing to myself here and I know that seems stupid, and I'm sure you'd say it IS stupid but it helps me think. Okay, like I've decided that I'm going to tell everybody the truth whether they believe me or not. I have to. I have no other choice. Like I couldn't live with myself if I didn't at least give the adults a chance to get you guys out. It's not like I'd be able to rescue you guys. No way, no how. I guess I always wished I could be that sort of person, a person like Emily, but I'm not. I don't look perfect like her and like you've told me over and over I'm a coward. I don't have a spine. What am I saying? That isn't news to you, is it? You, of all people, know what a coward I am. I'm not going near the shed—let alone the safe or that horrible bug book. I just hope you're all okay, and that Mom and Dad or somebody will be able to get you out alive so you can be able to hate me for many years to come.

Janice

• •

Date: April 1, 2005 **Time:** 11:24 p.m. CST.
From: JaniceJin@surftwn.comp
To: JaniceJin@surftwn.comp
Subject: *I've lost my mind*

E-mail from me to me? YES. Like, I'm afraid if I don't write down what has happened to me over the last several hours, I'll forget the details or worse yet, when I "go back" I won't get out and no one will ever know. I figure Emily's parents will check her computer files, eventually…

I wasn't planning on going near that book, no way, but at the Lockhardt's house, everybody is so crazy with grief and worry, that I felt like I must at least take a peek at it. Like I just can't explain why I did it. I was tired of being holed up in the bathroom for one, and I felt like it was out of my hands. I had to see the book. I had to touch it.

Ok like I'd only been in their shed once or twice, but I found the safe no problem. I felt a strange rush of fear and pain and believe it or not…recognition. I sensed that my brother and his friends were close by.

Slowly, I reached inside its dark walls until my fingers grazed paper. The bug book. I must admit, I thought about pulling my hand out and racing inside for safety—but only for a second.

Soon, I was holding the dreaded book in my hands. There wasn't a trace of the slime Joel had spoken of before. Was he messing with me? Actually, it looked harmless enough—at first. But as I sat on that same old crate that Joel had Mom sit on, and turned those first few pages, I realized this wasn't a regular, normal book after all.

Like if you looked really closely, you really could see the bugs quivering upon each page. Not like they were frightened of me or anything. Oh, no, quite the opposite. They looked like they were quivering with anticipation. Anticipation of the possible attack of yet another kid, namely me. I can't explain how I knew what they were thinking, but I knew it as clearly as I knew my own name— Queen of Mean. Like thanks for that sweet nickname Joel…Ok like anyway all those millions of bugs were excited. At first, it filled me with fear and dread, but then, well, then as I was scouring the pages, searching for Joel and Bud and Emily, worrying about whether they were even alive, it changed. I got mad. Real mad. Madder than I have ever been. Madder than I was when my parents moved to California. Madder than I was when Joel accidentally(?) dropped his bowling ball on my foot. (Although I was plenty mad.) Sitting in that shed, my pulse raced, my face reddened, my hands quivered, my whole body did too. I was shocked to realize that I wanted to get my hands on the awful little things. I wanted to squish them, make them suffer, for putting Joel and my folks (and me) through hell. I saw it out of the corner of my eye. It was closed, in the corner. Joel's laptop. I picked it up and tucked it under my shirt. What was I doing?

I resumed my spot on the crate by the safe and waited. It wasn't long before I heard the clicking. It was so loud. Then I saw what must have been hundreds of little legs marching out of the safe towards me. I admit I cowered, I felt like I had to go to the bathroom but I didn't move. I don't think I could have anyway.

The bugs—I don't know what kind cause I've never seen them before—literally lifted me up and everything got all misty for me, but I do remember the feeling of…evaporating. That's the only way I know how to put it. I was like fading away. It was very bizarre. Like I knew I was headed into the dangerous unknown of the pages of that book. I knew I had a huge battle before me—unlike anything I'd ever faced. Then as if I were drugged, everything was spinning around me. I remember the feel of the glossy pages upon my skin and the smell of glue and shiny paper. I remember the feeling of being "sucked in" by the book, I remember seeing flashes of green and blue, white, black—suffocating black—while being dropped into this strange world. That's all I remembered before I blacked out...

chapter Eighteen

From: JaniceJin@surftwn.comp
To: JaniceJin@surftwn.comp *(Continued)*

When I woke up, (with Joel's laptop pushing against my ribs) I found myself lying on a soft warm bed of grass in a world that was like, prettier than Emily. The sun's rays took me into their arms. Like I literally was getting a solar hug. It was so awesome. AWESOME. Oh, and I saw flowers of brilliant colors—purples, plums, and the most effervescent pinks—just breath-taking. Awesome. Off in the distance stood the greenest of green trees, lavish with thick foliage, and to top it all off, a sparkling river whispered nearby. At first I was so blown away by the beauty of it all, I literally forgot who I was—and where I was. Wow. I *loved* forgetting who I was and where I was. I wish I still didn't know. Knowing has not been fun. Not knowing was sweet. So sweet…

The seemingly harmless sound of crickets is what jolted me back to reality—whatever that is. I heard them, but couldn't see them. I bolted upright, and called for Joel. Nothing. I called for Bud and then for Emily. Nothing. I looked around at this wonderland I had entered, and shook my head sadly. How was it possible that such horrible bugs could inhabit such an awesome world? How was it that my brother and his friends as well as my own life could be in danger here? Sweat dripped from my temples, and I pushed up the sleeves of my wool sweater and walked toward the sound of water. I was incredibly thirsty. Parched, actually. The temperature had to be close to 100 degrees. Worried, but still entranced with this beautiful place inside such a horrific book, I plodded along, all the while calling out for Joel.

Joel didn't answer, but someone else did. I heard him in the distance, weakly calling out Emily's name. It was Bud. Like, seriously, my heart flip-flopped. If Bud was okay, Joel must be too! I raced toward the sound of his voice, but still not having found him, I yelled for Bud to keep talking so I could track him down.

Bud yelled back for me to stop and not come any closer. His voice suddenly had a new volume and urgency and fear—enough fear to stop me dead in my tracks.

I asked him where he was and what was going on, but I didn't move.

I heard him say something like, "here I'm over here." I craned to see him. I shielded my eyes from the sun and turned a full 360 degrees—and then some. Still, I saw nothing. "Up here, Janice," the voice said.

I looked about twenty yards away, squinting at a figure waving from inside the crook of a giant oak tree. The figure was dark blonde, wearing jeans and hanging on for dear life. Like it was Bud, all right.

Of course I raced towards him, but his voice once again stopped me in my tracks.

He screamed for me to stop and told me that THEY were right in front of me all over the place. He ordered me to turn around and go back.

I asked him what was all over? I was frustrated and mad and scared like all at the same time.

It skittered up my pant leg and even before I looked down, I knew what it was. I lowered my head until my gaze met that of a huge scorpion—the size of my fist. It seemed to grimace at me as it bent back its tail in anger and defiance. It was about to strike. I kicked my leg up so fast, it even shocked me, and that awful little creature flew off, landing in the meadow behind me.

"Hurry!" Bud yelled. He told me to get out of there while I still could, to run with all I had. I knew I'd be no use to anybody unless I had something—some sort of weapon—to fight these creatures so I turned and did just as Bud had told me to do. I yelled out to Bud, pointing to the ground where I'd set the computer down. I ran to the grassy spot I'd originally woken up on and searched for a way out. I saw an edge of blackness, blocks away and raced towards it. I was dripping with sweat, literally dripping, and I remember wondering how I was supposed to be able to get out of here. I started chanting, let me out...let me out...let me out...and then I raced into the black unknown. It was like running into an abyss of nothingness. That's all I remember.

The next thing I knew, I was on the floor of the Lockhardt's shed, right next to the safe, with the book clutched in my hands. I dropped it and let out a small screech. I wanted to scream. I wanted to scream until my voice couldn't scream anymore but I knew I couldn't do it because the adults would hear me, even out here, and come running. I now know that the bug book is literally a world unto itself. A world where bugs are the rulers and people are the servants. A book where terrorizing children is the main pastime. A world I never, EVER want to see again.

I am going back in there, and I'm not coming out without my brother, Bud and Emily.

Janice

• •

Date: April 1, 2005 **Time:** 11: 44 p.m. CST.
To: JaniceJin@surftwn.comp
From: Elockhardt@wryword.comp
Subject: *Hey Janice! THANKS!*

Janice, I can't believe that Joel and you came inside this horrible book to try and save us. Especially you. I don't mean to be mean but I didn't know you had it in you. Joel and you are incredibly brave. We can't thank you enough for being smart enough to bring Joel's laptop computer in here. Now at least we have a way we can communicate with the outside world.

You know, when I look back over the last few days, I can hardly believe what I'm remembering—was it real, Janice? Is it?

I remember when Bud told us he saw you, coming toward him in that tree. We were completely floored. Completely. We couldn't imagine that you would've found your way inside that book. But you sure did.

Janice, we don't know where Joel is. The last time we saw him we were all running away from a huge mass of stinging beetles. Bud got stung a couple of times in his right leg. It's all swollen up. At least he has his inhaler, now, but Janice, it still doesn't look too good. I'm so scared. This is too much to bear now—Bud being hurt—plus being apart from Joel—not knowing if he's hurt or…

Bud and I are living moment to moment, scrounging for these weird orange berries and taking turns sleeping while the other keeps watch for bugs and Joel. Bud can't really move very fast. His asthma is bothering him too—even with the inhaler. Janice, I think the inhaler is running out, but he doesn't complain; I just hear it in his breathing.

We're pretty much stuck here. Right now it looks like we're on page 118—some jungle or other. It's very hot and very buggy—but for now these bugs seem to be of the normal variety. They're not attacking us—at least for the moment.

It's so hard to believe that we're actually stuck in here. Janice, if you did get out…how did you do it? What did you do? Please e-mail us back and let us know.

Em

• •

Date: April 1, 2005 **Time:** 11: 50 p.m. CST.
To: JaniceJin@surftwn.comp
From: Elockhardt@wryword.comp
Subject: *Re: Hey Janice! THANKS!*

Yeah, Emily, I got out. Like I don't know how I was able to escape—I only know that if *willing it to happen* is possible, then that's what I did.

I went back to the spot I like "dropped in" and looked around. I saw darkness and raced into it. The next thing I remember I was on the shed floor.

Oh please find Joel. Please. You've got to—for his sake and for your own sakes. He's got all the weapons. Didn't he show you them before?

Janice

• •

Date: April 1, 2005 **Time:** 11:52 p.m. CST.
To: JaniceJin@surftwn.comp
From: Elockhardt@wryword.comp
Subject: *Re: Hey Janice! THANKS!*

No, he didn't show us anything. Right after he arrived in the book, some huge bugs chased us down—I don't know what they were. I think I remember Joel carrying something—like a backpack—but I can't be sure.

I think I will have to leave Bud in this cave we found and go off searching for Joel. I don't know what else to do.

I hope—

Janice. I heard a large swooshing sound, turned around and Bud was gone. GONE. It's so thick with fog and foliage in here I can't see much of anything. I don't know what took Bud, but something did.

I'm alone now Janice. Alone in this bug world. Help me. HELP ME!!

Em

chapter Nineteen

Date: April 1, 2005 **Time:** 11:55 p.m. CST.
From: JaniceJin@surftwn.comp
To: Elockhardt@wryword.comp
Subject: *Re: Hey Janice! THANKS!*

I AM going to try and help you, Emily. I'm going to come back inside that book as soon as I can. But, it's been impossible to do that so far because I'm being watched. My parents really sense that I'm up to something and have ordered me to stay inside from now on. I think they saw me leaving the shed and think I'm losing it. Or maybe they can "feel" that something evil is lurking out there. Whatever reason neither of them will let me near it.

Right now Mom's sitting across the room, (pretending to read the paper) but like, really, she's watching me type this. She follows me everywhere! She even knocks on the door of the bathroom if I'm in there longer than a minute or two. Between Mom and Grandma I've got no privacy to do anything around here. I guess you can't blame her, she's *sooo* worried about you all, but geez, it's hard. I'm still planning on getting back in the book. I'm just letting you know what's up. Right now, while I'm e-mailing you I'm trying to look calm. Calm? Ha. I don't think I'll ever feel calm again, as long as I live. But I think I can look calm. I have to. I told her I'm e-mailing Sally (my best friend in California). She believes me…I think.

Emily, you must stay calm—or as close to it as you can find. Unlike me, the truth is you are strong. You've made it this far. Now is NOT the time to give up and panic. You must say a prayer, (Joel told me you pray lots) I think I might give that a try too. Also, take a deep, deep breath and decide what to do next. You have the logical ability to save yourself AND Bud and Joel, Emily. YOU DO. You must believe that…because it's true. You have the power. Talk about girl power? EMILY POWER!

But that doesn't mean you shouldn't be careful. You must still be very careful. Like after all the years I've known you, this is the first time I've ever sort of liked you. So don't go and spoil it by dying, okay? You can bring everybody back, Emily, I'm sure of it. I'm here if you need me, (and hopefully I'll be able to be there soon).

Janice

P.S. I just realized that today is April 1st—like as in April Fools Day. Wouldn't it be awesome if that were all this was? A huge buggy joke that wasn't real?

• •

Date: April 1, 2005 **Time:** 11:59 p.m. CST.
To: JaniceJin@surftwn.comp
From: Elockhardt@wryword.comp
Subject: *Re: Hey Janice! THANKS!*

If only it was just an April Fools prank. But it's not. And you're right, Janice. I can't fall apart now—I'll wait until I get home to do it. As for praying? I've prayed more these last few days than I've ever prayed in my life. I even told God that if he got us out of this, I would promise to pray tons even when things were going great. If God was looking to get me into the regular prayer habit, it worked. Oh, Janice, I must figure out a way to find Bud and Joel and then get us out of here. First off, I think I'm going to head back to Page 115 in the bug book—that's where I first spotted Joel. He might still be there or maybe at least his backpack might still be lying around. If I can get a hold of the weapons you said he brought, I'd have a much better shot at getting us all out alive.

But Janice, this is serious—I don't want you to come back—it wouldn't do any good for another one of us to be stuck here. You can help us much better by being where you are…I MEAN IT.

Now that I've eaten the last of those orange berry-like things, I guess I should try and get some sleep. I'm on the cicada page. Their shiny black and green bodies are everywhere. They haven't tried to hurt me at all, thank heavens, but boy, are they loud! There are so many of them, crawling around the floor of the forest, and they are quite large, so it's hard not to get freaked out.

I could try and sleep in a tree, but why? There are just as many of them up there. Besides, it's hard for my body to adjust to sleeping much, since it never gets dark (on this page). I'll sleep in the most sheltered area I can find. Here, it looks like my bed will be the foot of an oak tree. No caves or soft hay here. Tomorrow morning I'll go to Page 115 to search for Joel. Wish me luck. If I remember right, I think that's where the tarantulas are…

Em

Date: April 2, 2005 **Time:** 12:23 a.m. CST.
To: JaniceJin@surftwn.comp
From: Elockhardt@wryword.comp
Subject: *Re: Hey Janice! THANKS!*

Janice, I had no idea how difficult it would be to tra-verse from page to page. I've only been "carried" by the bugs before—this was a whole new ball game. Very weird. I traveled for maybe a ½ a mile to the edge of the woods and found that they literally just stop and there is nothing beyond. It is so bizarre, I just don't know how to get across to you how strange it is to be standing beneath these huge massive trees, literally buzzing with life and look just a foot away and see complete blackness. I wonder if this is what dying feels like...

It took all the courage I could grab to move forward into the total unknown, blindly searching for a way out. Soon I was down on all fours crawling, then squiggling like a snake, using my full body weight to move, the weight of the book constricting me; it went *sooooo* slowly. It was there I could tell that I was actually stuck inside a book. I could literally feel the smooth glossiness of the paper on my front and my back as I struggled, hoping to find a way to make it to the weapons Joel left on page 115.

I had the laptop secured under my shirt and its sharp edges ravaged me unrelentingly with each movement I made. I was tempted to pull it out and leave it behind, but I knew that would be nuts. This is my only connection to the "outside world" I have right now, and I am not givin' it up—no way, no how.

So, I kept pushing along, glorified worm that I was, and suddenly I saw it: a room. It was dark, but I could still make out objects. My breath literally left my body as I realized what I was seeing. Our dark, stinky shed. I gazed at Mom's hoe with awe. It was one of the most beautiful things I'd ever seen in my life. It always will be. I realized I was half in, half out of that book, and that all I'd need to do is push my way forward instead of bending back around to page 115, and I would be out. I was very small, and the shed looked very big, and I don't know how long it was that I looked around, devouring my surroundings, if you will, knowing all along that I couldn't leave Bud and Joel, so I lifted the next page and dove back in.

Now that I think of it, I'm sure I was only able to get out on that page because the cicadas had left me alone. Had I been on a different page...I believe it would have been much more difficult—if not impossible.

I haven't seen anything here but a couple of tarantulas, which, thankfully, looked surprised to see me and quickly skittered off as I walked. I'm sure that won't last. It won't be long until they collaborate and come after me. I have very little time. In fact, the only reason I took the time to e-mail you was to tell you not to give up your hopes. Bud and Joel might be on a page they can actually escape from. Listen for them, or me, huh?

I'm off to search for the weapons...I sure hope they're worth searching for...

Em

chapter Twenty

Date: April 2, 2005 **Time:** 1:26 a.m. CST.
To: JaniceJin@surftwn.comp
From: Elockhardt@wryword.comp
Subject: *Re: Hey Janice! THANKS!*

I found Joel's backpack. It's amazing that I found it at all, because it was lying in the long marsh grasses. Truth is, I tripped over it. It was open and pretty soggy, but the stuff he'd stuffed inside was still okay: a flashlight, a half-empty can of bug killer, about 12 of those little poisonous bug motel thingies and a pair of scissors. Bug motels and a pair of scissors? Janice, what was Joel thinking? That while the bugs were checking in to the motel he was going to grab 'em in the lobby, then methodically sit down and one by one cut each bug in two? There was something else in here too, but I have no idea what it is or what it's here for. I gotta go, I hear rustling behind me…oh no, it looks like a huge black carpet moving towards me. It's the tarantulas…

Em

• •

Date: April 2, 2005 **Time:** 2:09 a.m. CST.
From: JaniceJin@surftwn.comp
To: Elockhardt@wryword.comp
Subject: *WHERE ARE YOU?*

Emily, are you okay? Emily, let me know. Please. Like it's so hard to sit here not knowing what's going on. Let me know as soon as you can.
Janice

• •

Date: April 2, 2005 **Time:** 2:23 a.m. CST.
To: JaniceJin@surftwn.comp
From: Elockhardt@wryword.comp
Subject: *Re: WHERE ARE YOU?*

I'm okay; I ran away and kept going. I was so scared. I was so close to getting bitten. I found this shelter. It's dark here, Janice. I mean darker than any dark on earth. Am I still on earth? Technically, maybe, but not really. I am on a different "earth" within a book on my usual earth. This is too weird. Too weird. Oh. There's a huge spider web over there. Man, taller than Dad. My voice echoes…Eeewww, I think I'm in their cave. My eyelids hurt. I mean it. They feel like they weigh as much as my thighs. I just can't sleep, though.

I think I slept, I'm not sure. It's hard to know because this all feels too unreal in the first place. If I was sleeping, it was a beautiful dream. It felt real, but it couldn't have been because it wasn't horrible, it was wonderful. I was sitting in a field of the brightest daisies—and also these little purple flowers that smelled like…well, like heaven. Wow, I can still smell a trace of them in my memory now. I just sat there for the longest time, breathing it all in—the scent surrounded me like a comforter. It was so lightly sweet and warm. I felt happy. Really happy. Sublime. I've never used that word before, but it fits. I felt sublime. I couldn't help it.

Then the most beautiful butterfly I've ever seen—that you could ever even think of—floated towards me. I cringed at first—I'm conditioned to do that now, I guess. But the lavender and gold-striped creature hovered around me for a minute or two and then softly landed on my knee. It looked up at me, Janice. Right into my eyes. I could not look away, even if I had wanted to. The truth is, I didn't want to. I then felt a feeling of peace like I have never felt before—not even before all of this bug nightmare started. I felt like peace was something that could really happen for the whole world someday. The whole galaxy. The whole everything that's anywhere. Janice, I felt for a moment like I could fly. I *believed* I could fly, and that it wouldn't be a big deal to do it, either. The wings of the butterfly rose and fell in beautiful, rhythmic succession as the creature hovered in front of my face. I swear, Janice, it was not only staring at me; it was smiling. Smiling. So was I. Slowly, it turned around and flew off above the meadow until it was out of sight. It was then I realized that I was not sitting on the ground. Janice, I was sitting in the air—floating in the air, just like that butterfly had. As soon as I realized my jeans were not on solid soil, I hit the ground with a huge thump. (My rear still hurts, but it was worth it.) It was a dream, right? This bug world couldn't possibly have anything so beautiful within it...right?

Em

• •

Date: April 2, 2005 **Time:** 3:06 a.m. CST.
From: JaniceJin@surftwn.comp
To: Elockhardt@wryword.comp
Subject: *Re: WHERE ARE YOU?*

Wow, like that's awesome Emily. I'm happy that you had some time in the book where you weren't frightened and worried—even if it was while you were sleeping. If you were sleeping. Like just reading about it made ME feel more at peace. It must have been incredible. Hey, if you were sleeping, why would your, er, butt ache?

Anyway, I'm so glad that you're okay and that you found Joel's backpack. To tell you the truth, I'm not quite sure what Joel had in mind by including scissors. Maybe it was the only pointed object he could find at the time…If they're coming after you and if you have to stab them or whatever, then do it with the scissors I guess.

Emily I think you need to keep moving. I think as long as you can stay one step ahead of those buggers you can stay safe. Right?

What else did Joel put in his backpack? Maybe I can help you figure out what it is and why my brother put it there? Maybe not. But let me give it a shot.

Janice

• •

Date: April 2, 2005 **Time:** 4:56 a.m. CST.
To: JaniceJin@surftwn.comp
From: Elockhardt@wryword.comp
Subject: *Re: WHERE ARE YOU?*

This is too much, Janice. I'm scared. I hear something and it's scurrying and it's big. It has to be big to be that loud.

It sounds like it's coming towards me. I need that can of bug
ki

• •

Date: April 2, 2005 **Time:** 5:07 a.m. CST.
To: JaniceJin@surftwn.comp
From: Elockhardt@wryword.comp
Subject: *Re: WHERE ARE YOU?*

Janice, you're not going to believe this, but I just nailed
Bud in the knee with bug killer. Yes, you read it right. I found
Bud! A huge mess of gnats or something took him, but he
says he thinks they got tired of holding onto him and dumped
him off about an hour ago. Boy, was I happy to see him and
boy, was he happy to see me, too. We actually hugged. I've
been hugging and praying so much lately; it's getting hard to
recognize myself.

But Janice, Joel isn't in here with us. The last time Bud
saw him was on page 124. So…you guessed it. Bud and I are
headed back to 124 in the bug book. I'll e-mail you as soon
as I find anything out. If we can get away from the tarantulas,
they are coming towards us right now. Bud is layin' on the
bug killer…

Em

• •

Date: April 2, 2005 **Time:** 6:54 a.m. CST.
To: JaniceJin@surftwn.comp
From: Elockhardt@wryword.comp
Subject: *Re: WHERE ARE YOU?*

We're out of the cave now, but just barely—we left the
empty can of bug killer in there, along with about a dozen

dead tarantulas. What are we going to do without that bug spray? I don't want to think about it. This is hard to believe but we're hungry. How can we be hungry at a time like this? But we are. We've been able to drink the dew off of leaves and found some puddles so we aren't too thirsty anymore, but boy, are we starving. Mom's turkey meatloaf even sounds good right now.

We're sitting right outside the cave, right towards the end of the page and there is nothing to eat here. Bud says that there is plenty to eat on page 124—where we think Joel is—but there are also probably deadly bugs there. Of course we're going anyway—BECAUSE Joel is probably still there. Bud said Joel's legs were pretty badly bitten, and that it looked like they might be getting infected. That's why we figure he couldn't have gone too far. Both Bud and I *feel* like Joel is still okay. We don't know why, but we do, and that seems to be enough to keep us going. Gosh Janice, I miss Joel so much, but it sure helps having Bud here…and *you* there. I'll e-mail you from page 124—I hope…

Em

P.S. Oh my God, Janice, Bud just squealed—he was in the cave doing his business and you won't believe what he found: Peter Schwann. He was woven inside the back of that huge spider web I told you about. He weakly called out to Bud or we never would have seen him. Bud got him out just before the MASSIVE, black tarantula came back to the web. He said the fangs on that thing were a foot long each. Peter must have been passed out before when I was in there. He's SO weak, Janice. It looks like he's lost about half of himself and that was a lot to lose! He's almost kind of thin. We're going to have to find him some berries—and fast. I just can't believe any of this is happening. I wish Mom would come in and wake me up. Is this all a nightmare, Janice? Please tell me it is. Please. Don't bother. I know it's real. It's far too real. At least we found Peter and he's still okay. But will that last? Will we last? We've got to get away from that tarantula that took Peter. Bud says he heard it hiss…

• •

Date: April 2, 2005 **Time:** 7:29 a.m. CST.
To: JaniceJin@surftwn.comp
From: Elockhardt@wryword.comp
Subject: *Not looking good*

Peter, Bud and I tried to leave the page but we can't, and Janice, things are pretty bad. Those blasted termites all of the sudden popped up and they are everywhere. EVERYWHERE. They're all over Peter, Bud, the laptop and me—they're covering it. I continuously have to push their bodies off my face and the keyboard and screen after every few words. Thankfully, I was able to eat some of those weird orange berries before they moved in. We fed Peter first. Bud was busy setting up our "arsenal" so he barely got in a few bites before they descended on the fruit and on us. They ate it all. All of it. There isn't one full berry left…Pigs!!! I thought termites were only supposed to eat wood. We are still so hungry…Peter isn't, though. He says his stomach is upset now. I think he went so long without food/water that his body is having a problem accepting it now.

Peter doesn't remember every detail, but what he does remember is creepy. He remembers being on his way to school and hearing something coming up from behind him. He was sure it was one of the neighborhood kids, but it wasn't. The next thing he knows he was flipped up and over—landing on top of a slew of tarantulas. He remembers how coarse their body hairs felt on his body—his neck, especially. He kept saying how their legs all moved precisely at the same time. It was like it was some strange dance number or something. He doesn't remember them bringing him inside the book. He does remember hearing me and Bud talking about the book and what we were going to do, and he remembers calling out to us, but he said we never seemed to hear him. He said he thought about his whole life while he was trapped between our world and the bug world and he realized that he wasn't ready to just disappear into the book and be chalked up as a runaway. He realized he had a lot more he wanted to do with his life but now it's too late. I didn't have the heart to tell him that he was probably right.

Peter has seen things that we haven't, Janice. I don't know how to put this, but he said he's seen things…We asked what kind of things and he started to talk but had to stop. He kept swallowing over and over and put his head down. Finally, he said when he first got here he was running around, trying to avoid bugs and looking for a way out. He climbed a tree to see if he could get better perspective. He said he could see for miles and it looked like the ground was moving, because it was. He compared it to a huge herd of gazelles or elephants in Africa, only the herd was of the bug variety and they were coming towards him. They were like the size of grasshoppers he said, but he also said he'd never seen bugs like that before. They were almost flesh colored and it appeared that some of them would periodically pause to communicate with each other. While he was in the tree he saw something glinting in the sunshine. It was soft and silky. He shoved it into his pocket and has shown it to me. Janice, it's a hair ribbon. A bright red hair ribbon—the type that we used to wear when we were younger. Whose ribbon is that? Have there been other kids here before us? If so, where are they now? WHERE? There are other things, too. Pieces of polyester fabric—stuck on thorn bushes—it looks like whoever was wearing it was running wildly to get away from the bugs and their clothes ripped and shoes. Little kids sandals, an older girl's loafer, where are they now? Peter told Bud that there was some writing on the walls of the cave and Bud is insisting on going back in to see it. That tarantula is still in there! Bud won't back down, though; he says this might be a clue to what is going on and how to get back out of this book. So Peter and I are going to try and lure the creature away so Bud can check and see. Wish us luck…

Darnit! I was so freaked out, I left the computer on! There can't be much battery life left now, thanks to my stupidity. But, Janice, we did it! Got the spider away (I screamed and flailed and spit at it—and then ran into a thick patch of woods. It couldn't get through them and that really ticked it off), and Bud found the writing. The only problem is, as Bud so aptly put it "I don't speak freakin' hieroglyphics."

I couldn't believe it, but he said that's exactly what it looks like—like something out of an old history book—something written millions of years ago. Why would there be Egyptian writings on the cave wall in the bug book? How could there be? How long has all of this been going on, Janice? Who all has been inside here? Who is STILL here?

When Bud was walking out of the cave he noticed something else scratched onto the cave wall right by the entrance. It said something like, "Johnny Abrams, 1969…" Huh? Egyptian times to the 1960's to 2,000—plus? How many kids have been in here? Is that Johnny kid still here somewhere? He'd be an adult now. I just can't worry about that though—there are so many termites; it is really incomprehensible. They are lined up over ten feet high in a solid wall right near the end of the page. I'm telling you: They *know* we've been traveling from page to page and they *know* how, and they are making sure we will never get out of here. Janice, it is a quivering, buzzing wall of bug bodies, so solidly packed together, it may as well be concrete.

Janice, there is no way out. No way at all. We're stuck.

Em

chapter Twenty-one

Date: April 2, 2005 **Time:** 10:46 a.m. CST.
From: JaniceJin@surftwn.comp
To: Elockhardt@wryword.comp
Subject: *Re: Not looking good*

Emily, like try and stay calm. I can't believe all the stuff you're telling me but I have to, cause I was there and saw it with my own eyes. It's incredible. The mere thought of that book taking in children for any amount of time let alone thousands or millions of years is just unbearable. The book has to be crushed to like smithereens. I'm not completely sure what smithereens are, but like I know that's what needs to happen to the book, anyway. I know you're desperate right now with the termites. I think that what you need to do is figure out how to distract the termites or something. Think. What's the other thing in the backpack, Emily? You haven't told me yet. Since you don't have any bug killer left, you gotta use what you still DO have. Are you and Bud OK?

Janice

• •

Date: April 2, 2005 **Time:** 11:16 a.m. CST.
To: JaniceJin@surftwn.comp
From: Elockhardt@wryword.comp
Subject: *Re: Not looking good*

Bud is wheezing pretty badly, must have been a bunch of mold in the cave. He's always been pretty allergic to that stuff. He tried to use his inhaler again, but nothing was left. He tossed it away. I'm worried about him and Peter. I'm okay, just tired and kinda dizzy, well, sometimes REALLY dizzy. I guess it's 'cause I'm weak being hungry and all, not to mention lack of sleep. We're not giving up, that's for sure.

Janice, I haven't told you about the last thing in the backpack because it is so ridiculous. I have no idea what Joel was thinking…It's a can of spray starch. Yes, you read it right—SPRAY STARCH. What the heck am I supposed to do with that? The bugs, laundry, for crying out loud? Gotta go, these termites are marching up my legs.

Em

. . . .

Date: April 2, 2005 **Time:** 11:21 a.m. CST.
From: JaniceJin@surftwn.comp
To: Elockhardt@wryword.comp
Subject: *Re: Not looking good*

Emily, shut-up! This is NOT <u>IT</u>. That was brilliant of Joel to stick in that starch. Think. All you and Bud have to do is wait for the right moment, spray a part of the bug wall with the starch then toss their petrified little bodies out of the way and go find Joel.

Janice

. . . .

Date: April 2, 2005 **Time:** 11:49 a.m. CST.
To: JaniceJin@surftwn.comp
From: Elockhardt@wryword.comp
Subject: *Re: Not looking good*

Yeah, right. Do you have any idea how BIG their wall is? How many termites we're talking about here?

Em

• •

Date: April 2, 2005 **Time:** 12:02 p.m. CST.
From: JaniceJin@surftwn.comp
To: Elockhardt@wryword.comp
Subject: *Re: Not looking good*

You only need a small space to slither through. Like, spray the critters and then when they harden get them out of the way. If you move quickly enough you all should be able to pass through.

Emily, I think that you should drop the backpack and laptop onto Page 124 for Joel, and then you should come out of the book once and for all. I am positive he wouldn't want you and Bud endangering yourselves anymore for him. Having the Queen of Mean endanger herself is another story. ;-) You guys are all beat up as it is and you might not get the chance to get out again. And, like, what about Peter? This could be his last chance to make it out alive.

Listen. That is what you MUST do. If you leave the computer and supplies, I WILL get in and take over. Like I'm rested and as Joel would attest, perpetually over-fed. I would last eons in there.

Janice

• •

Date: April 2, 2005 **Time:** 12:29 p.m. CST.
To: JaniceJin@surftwn.comp
From: Elockhardt@wryword.comp
Subject: *Re: Not looking good*

NO. I am not taking off and leaving an injured Joel with just a laptop, bug motels and a can of ironing aide. I will not!! And YOU, Janice are not coming back in, either. Enough of us have been in danger. It's got to stop. It's got to STOP! This is all my fault, really. If it weren't for that stupid bug report, we wouldn't all be in this mess. Actually, now that I think of it, it's really that old, old—OLD Mrs. Robbins fault, if she hadn't meanly ASSIGNED me that stupid bug report none of this would have happened.

Wait a minute. Yes it would have. Bud would have still had the book. Why am I wasting time blaming my teacher for something she had nothing to do with? Haven't I learned anything? I feel like my mind is on overload—like an electrical socket with way too many things plugged in.

I would give anything right now for a diet cola. Over ice. With lemon—it's carbonation coming back through my nose. I want to gulp it down and taste the tartness and sweetness and then I want to let out the biggest burp of my life. Right while I'm sitting, smack-dab, in the front row of decrepit Mrs. Robbins class—*ack!* There I go again! What's wrong with me, Janice? I've got to get a grip.

Okay, back to reality. Ha. That's funny. Reality. IS this reality? If it is, I'd rather be dreaming. Or, am I already dre—

Enough. I just slapped myself. I swear I did. It worked. I think. Janice, I am going to send Peter and Bud out. Bud

131

refuses (of course), but I have a plan and I need you to help me with it: I am going to lead us to the edge of the book and then tell Bud to go first. I'll pretend we're all going back to page 124 to look for Joel. Janice, when Bud is just about at the top of the page, ready to dive back into page 124, I am going to give him a shove and I need you to be there to give his arm a yank, and pull him out of the book altogether.

He is barely able to breathe anymore (his asthma is sooo bad in here) and I'm afraid that whatever mold—or whatever it is—that lies on page 124 could literally take his breath away for good. I'll shove Peter through next.

Janice, we can't waste anymore time. We have to try your spray starch idea NOW. The wall of termites is thickening every second. If all goes well, Joel and I will be e-mailing you and Bud from page 124. If not, well, if not, then we won't.

The computer screen is fading somewhat and I've noticed that there's a little icon doohickey signaling that it's losing power and so are the rest of us. I'm afraid there isn't much time left…

Em

• •

Date: April 2, 2005 **Time:** 2:39 p.m. CST.
To: JaniceJin@surftwn.comp
From: Elockhardt@wryword.comp
Subject: *Uh-oh. How mad is he?*

Em

• •

Date: April 2, 2005 **Time:** 2:41 p.m. CST.
To: Elockhardt@wryword.comp
From: JaniceJin@surftwn.comp
Subject: *Re: Uh-oh. How mad is he?*

I'm REAL MAD! How dare you pull a stunt like that, Em. Shoving your older brother out of there like I'm some little kid—and getting Janice of all people to help you? I am not going to forgive you for this so you better hurry up and get out of there so I can make the rest of your LONG life miserable.

Man, oh man, you really are like some sort of wonder woman. All those years you've been telling me, Joel, the folks, your girlfriends, everyone you've ever met etc., that, but who knew it was actually true? It is, so keep staying strong, Em. You have to. Hang on. Where's Peter? Did you find Joel yet? How's the power on the laptop?

Bud

• •

Date: April 2, 2005 **Time:** 2:50 p.m. CST.
To: JaniceJin@surftwn.comp
From: Elockhardt@wryword.comp
Subject: *Re: Uh-oh. How mad is he?*

Bud, Peter refused to leave a girl to do a man's job. He's only hindering this whole thing, but he won't listen to me; he says it's all his fault we ended up here in the first place which, now that I think of it, is pretty much true. His and Mrs. Robbins, that is. (I just can't stop myself...)

Anyway, Peter's wavering back and forth on his feet as I write this. The guy can barely stand but he thinks he's going to be able to help. Oh, to top things off, the computer juice is just about gone, BUT the millipedes are not. It's back to where this whole nightmare started. What IS it with millipedes and me?

We've been bitten a couple of times while we were looking for Joel. Who knew millipedes bite? The ones that bite me keep following me, with all those icky little hairy legs. Hey, if I can't sleep, I'll just count the millipedes' legs. Ha. Oh, not funny, I guess. You know I feel like I've been in here forever. It's eerie but not scary. Not much is scary anymore.

Bud, I feel like I'm in a fog, a misty fog that gets deeper and deeper every minute. I feel like I want to lie down and sleep...for good. I won't even need to count the legs to do it. Is it over yet? Are we there yet? I could really go for some chocolate chip cookies. Peter was telling me that there are people that cook with and eat bugs. Like worms in cookies, for example. Gross, but I AM hungry...Am I rambling? Peter said I'm rambling. How does he know? It's not like I'm saying all this out loud.

Oh. Whaddya know? Peter just told me I <u>am</u> saying this out loud. I think that's the first (or second or third) sign that I'm losing it. Isn't it? Peter just nodded yes. Gee, he's hilarious.

Em

• •

Date: April 2, 2005 **Time:** 3:57 p.m. CST.
To: Elockhardt@wryword.comp
From: JaniceJin@surftwn.comp
Subject: *Snap out of it!*

I'm worried, Emily. You seem to be getting confused about what is going on and what you should be doing. You have to try and find Joel and get out of there. Like, this isn't the time to be thinking about cookies—bug filled or otherwise. Get a grip and move it out of there. Try!

Janice

●　●

Date: April 2, 2005 **Time:** 5:56 p.m. CST.
To: JaniceJin@surftwn.comp
From: Elockhardt@wryword.comp
Subject: *Re: Snap out of it!*

I can't breathe. I can't believe this. Janice, we saw a boy, kind of. It looked like another boy—a boy we don't know or recognize. We followed the sounds of a waterfall and he was sitting at the base of it, with his feet in the water. When he first saw us his eyes lit up but then he screamed out, "No!" And I mean screamed! It scared us plenty, I'll tell you that. We walked over to him (I slipped twice on the wet boulders) but eventually I made it there. Janice, he looks to be about 15 but swears he's 103. He's not joking—he says his name is Elmer and he talked about dust bowl and that he had a crush on some lass named Lila but he never got to tell her the extent of it. Yes, Dust Bowl, and he actually used the word "lass." What is going on? He's got wavy brown hair and a really nice smile. Bright and wide. He winked at me and I couldn't help giggling. He asked what year it was and we told him what year it was but he refused to believe it. He just shook his head and said that one day soon he will be leaving to go and find Lila. He said he would just have to survive on food stamps until he gets his life back in order. (Janice, what the heck are food stamps???) Then he slumped over and dropped his head into his hands.

135

It's sad because he said he knew he isn't going back to where he came from—but that he will be going where he belongs. They can't stop him from doing that...

Huh?

Anyway, we asked him if he's seen other kids in the book and he nodded. He told us that most of them are, er, gone now...(He looked around to make sure we were alone) and then said that they are working to pull more in. He talked about how they sent Angus out somewhere in the states but that he hadn't seen him back yet though. He was glad about that. Said Angus is a nasty buguy, whatever buguy means and told us to steer clear of him when he returns. He shook his head sadly and said, "You don't want nothing to do with Angus."

Peter dropped down beside the boy. "I think I already have," he said and he asked Elmer if Angus is skinny, hairy and freaky with greenish teeth and horrendously horrifiying breath.

In spite of the seriousness of the situation the boy/man smiled that wide, bright smile and said that yes, that's him all right. "Twas you he found, eh?" he asked Peter.

Peter nodded and looked so sad, Janice. He said that now, because of him there are innocent people trapped in here.

Elmer said "Hogwash," and told Peter that he didn't know what happened out there, but he did know that it isn't Peter's fault that you are in here. It isn't anyone's fault. Elmer said that Angus lures you in—been doing that for centuries.

Centuries? We all looked at each other with a growing sense of dread. "How? How could this be possible?" We asked him.

Elmer said that from what he'd gathered, it seems that it's the tarantulas are pretty much running the show—and that they've been on earth for over 22 million years. They've been busy spinning more than their webs all that time. "They done found a way to mix with the no-goods back when potions and curses were commonplace and prey on children whenever they could. They've mixed technological who-ha with ancient curse rites—and this is the result," Elmer said and snorted. He told us that's not all—they been in cohoots with the Egyptian Scarabs, too—and those smelly things already had power and magic in their corner.

Peter nodded. I didn't get it. "Scarabs?" I asked.

Peter told me that scarabs are a fancy name for dung beetles. I crinkled my nose. Yuck.

Peter said that ancient tests show that Egyptians were quite certain that scarabs just magically and suddenly manifested out of dung balls, and that the people related this to their own religious beliefs on resurrection and self-creation. They actually worshiped the things—had a special name for them even, Peter told us, but said he couldn't think of it.

Elmer could and he recited the individual letters: K, h, e, p, r, i. Khepri? Weird. Anyway Elmer told us that ancient Egyptian mythology held the scarab high as a symbol of creation, resurrection and never-ending life. They weren't so dumb, those Egyptians. "If it weren't for the scarabs the tarantulas wouldn't have been able to go as far as the creation of this book," Elmer said, adding, "call it a book, call it another world. Heck, go ahead and call it hell." He said that's what it is to him anyway. He told us that they've somehow been able to infuse themselves with the children in a way that is not pleasant—not pleasant at all. "Right now, it's just a few of us left—and of course, Angus here—" Elmer said, "plus, you guys and lovely lassies," (he said smiling at me). Lassies? My cheeks burned.

I asked him if that's what/who Angus is? And he 'yessum'ed in response.

"But what about you? How did you escape that same fate?" I asked Elmer.

He just sighed and let forth a laugh that had the hollowest sound I'd ever heard. Inch by inch he pulled his "feet" from the depths of the deep water. Our breathing halted in unison. Janice, He had 6 legs—they were dark, hairy and pointed. It wasn't until then that I noticed how long and thin his arms were in proportion to his body, too.

"I don't mean to frighten you," he said and told us it's almost done for him now, as we could see. He said that once the process is complete, he can leave.

"But how?" We asked him? How could he leave and go back to the world as a spider?

"I didn't say I was going to be able to go back to the earthly plain," he shared. Then he smiled and it was such a peaceful smile, Janice. It reminded me of that butterfly's smile. Elmer said, "Let's just say once my human body is transformed I'll be taking my soul and going back where I belong." Janice what he said next made my eyes water. He said that he knows he'll be seeing his girl there again, too. He just knows it. He winked at me again. How romantic is that?

We heard a loud squawk over the hill and suddenly Elmer's smile vanished and he cocked his head and motioned for us to duck down and be quiet.

We heard rustling atop the cliff overhead. Elmer leapt up the side of the cliff in no time and we could hear him talking with whatever/whoever was up there—but it wasn't in English—it wasn't in any kind of language we'd ever heard of. There was a series of chirps and whistles and low-pitched grunts. Soon, he was back down beside us.

Take heed, Elmer said and told us we gotta get out of there—and that we didn't have much time. He said he just got word that Angus is coming back any second.

Elmer pointed towards the grove of trees and hissed, "Run! Hurry!" We didn't need to be told twice. Peter and I started to run and then Elmer grabbed my arm. Part of me was freaked out, another part was confused. "Listen, young one," Elmer whispered into my ear. "You know what you've got to do when you get out of here, don't you?"

I looked into his eyes and noticed for the first time how dark black they were. I said, "You mean…?" and he nodded. He knew what I meant.

"But what about *you*?!" I asked him.

He smiled that incredible smile and said that he would be just fine, lass. "You heard me talking before," he said. You know I'll be doing just fine.

Janice, I think I do know that he'll be fine.

"Get going!" Elmer said, giving me a small push. "And remember to do as I say!" I promised him I would and I ran after Peter and wrote it all down to you. We are headed to find Joel now…

Em

• •

Date: April 2, 2005 **Time:** 7:39 p.m. CST.
To: JaniceJin@surftwn.comp
From: Elockhardt@wryword.comp
Subject: *Re: Snap out of it!*

Janice/Bud, we found Joel. But he's not looking too good. He was lying partially concealed under these bush things with huge blue green leaves. I would have walked right by him, if I hadn't heard him coughing. That's about all that he's able to do. He kinda half-said my name when I leaned down, but that's been it. His eyes haven't opened since; he's literally magenta with fever and his legs are twice the size of normal—they look like they could burst with infection.

He's dying. Joel's really dying. I think we all are…
Em

chapter Twenty-two

Date: April 2, 2005 **Time:** 8:28 p.m. CST.
From: JaniceJin@surftwn.comp
To: Elockhardt@wryword.comp
Subject: *Hang on, EM!*

Em, Janice is pretty shook up here, she keeps walking in circles mumbling, "Like, what can we do? Like, what can we do?" Like, what CAN we do, Em? LIKE this is crazy.

It's not just Joel and Peter who needs to get out of that book soon—so do you. What can we do, Em? What?? It is worse being out of the book when the people you care about are in it. It is worse. You've got to get out of there, Em, NOW!

Bud

• •

Date: April 2, 2005 **Time:** 8:33 p.m. CST.
To: JaniceJin@surftwn.comp
From: Elockhardt@wryword.comp
Subject: *Re: Hang on, EM!*

That's easier said than done, Bud. What am I supposed to do, carry the two of them right through this jungle floor of millipedes? I can't even see the edge of the page from here. I know you think I'm strong, but I know I'm not that strong.

Em

• •

Date: April 2, 2005 **Time:** 8:36 p.m. CST.
From: JaniceJin@surftwn.comp
To: Elockhardt@wryword.comp
Subject: *Re: Hang on, EM!*

Yes, you ARE that strong and that's exactly what you're
supposed to do. That's exactly what you HAVE to do. There's
no other alternative, Em. None. Get up, before you become
any weaker. Get up, pick up Joel and drag him towards the
edge. Then get Peter over there, too. Leave everything else.
Leave everything but your courage. You will need it, Em.
Janice and I will be right here waiting for you, ready to
help. We are going to sit right here until you come out. Do it
Em—DO IT NOW. Hurry, I know the folks will be coming
out here to the shed any minute. Janice said they are already
suspicious of her out here.

Bud

• •

Date: April 2, 2005 **Time:** 9:06 p.m. CST.
To: JaniceJin@surftwn.comp
From: Elockhardt@wryword.comp
Subject: *Re: Hang on, EM!*

Bud, that's the least of my worries. I can't do it; I just
can't. I haven't got any strength left. There are so many millipedes and they keep gnawing at us and slithering all over us.
It almost feels ticklish. Joel is so sick, and Peter and I are so
weak. The first thing Peter said when he saw me was, I want
my mommy. Huh? A sixteen-year-old boy/man admitting he
wants his mother? Joel started to cry and said he wanted his
mommy too.

142

That might be kind of funny in a different situation, but Bud, I had to admit that I wouldn't mind getting a hug from MY mommy either. What are we, babies? I feel like that right now. I miss Mom. I miss Dad. I miss you. Wow, life and death scenarios really peel away that thick shell of pretense, don't they? There just isn't time to mess around by pretending you don't need anybody or don't care what *they* think about you. We all need each other. It's really that simple, isn't it? What a hard way to learn that lesson, but it's a great lesson to learn. Anyway, I love you Buddy. You are the neatest brother I could have ever hoped for—I mean that. Truth is, I would have meant it even BEFORE any of this awful stuff happened, but of course, I would never have admitted it (see "outer shell, pretense stuff above ;-).

And Bud? Tell Janice that her bro "JJ" (who knew?) loves her, too. He's really come to rely on her, especially when they moved from Minnesota to California. Joel told me that Janice really started growing up once they hit the Pacific Ocean state. He admitted to me here that he can't imagine living there without her and he wouldn't want to. Tell her that, okay?

Tell Mom and Dad...tell Mom and Dad I'll see them in another time and place—and that in that special place Mrs. Robbins will be nowhere to be found. Tell them I'll be happy and smiling, and not in pain...or in trouble. I promise. I'll still be a stunning beauty, of course. That's a given. Oh and tell them I'm sorry that I completely screwed up that math test...As for that old, old, OLD Mrs. Robbins? Tell her that although, YES IT WAS HER FAULT, not to blame herself—but wait to tell her the last part for at least a week or after the first...

Bye Buddy Bud

Em

• •

Date: April 2, 2005 **Time:** 9:10 p.m. CST.
From: JaniceJin@surftwn.comp
To: Elockhardt@wryword.comp
Subject: *Re: Hang on, EM!*

You can tell them ALL yourself drama queen. You haven't called me buddy Bud since you were eight. Em, everything you wrote was real touching but there is something that I need to say to you: GET YOUR BUTT OFF OF THE GROUND. TELL PETER TO MOVE IT. GRAB HOLD OF JOEL, AND GET THE HECK OUT OF THERE—NOW. NOW!!!!! Or…are you a weak little quitter, Em? Is that what you REALLY are? Not the strong, smart, gorgeous woman that you've always told everyone you were?

Bud

• •

Date: April 2, 2005 **Time:** 10:54 p.m. CST.
To: JaniceJin@surftwn.comp
From: Elockhardt@wryword.comp
Subject: *Re: Hang on, EM!*

Gorgeous? Huh? That goes without saying? *Smart*? Bud, I'm stuck in a bug book. How *smart* can that be? And what do you mean *woman*? You wonder if I'm a strong *woman*? I'm no woman, Bud. I'm a 13-year-old *girl*. And I feel like I'm getting younger by the minute.

Em

chapter
Twenty-three

Date: April 2, 2005 **Time:** 10:59 p.m. CST
To: Elockhardt@wryword.comp
From: JaniceJin@surftwn.comp
Subject: *Re: Hang on, EM!*

This is bull. Stop screwing around and get out of there now!!!

Bud

• •

Date: April 2, 2005 **Time:** 11:07 p.m. CST.
To: JaniceJin@surftwn.comp
From: Elockhardt@wryword.comp
Subject: *Re: Hang on, EM!*

After your little ploy, I bet you thought I'd come charging out, Joel on my hip, saying something like, "Being a superwoman is no problemo for me…"

Well, guess what? I'm no strong woman, Bud. At my very best I'm a weak, little child and that's all I have the energy to be, that's all I ever will be, because I'm not going to make it out. The power on this thing is just about gone. I keep seeing warnings. Oh, and Buddy? Nice try though.

Em

● ●

Date: April 2, 2005 **Time:** 11:22 p.m. CST.
From: JaniceJin@surftwn.comp
To: Elockhardt@wryword.comp
Subject: *Re: Hang on, EM!*

You are the most selfish person I've ever known. Go ahead and give up! GIVE UP!!!!!!!!!!!! I'm ashamed of you, Em. When push comes to shove you choose to lie down and die! So you won't be married in the St. Paul Cathedral, you won't have that big writing/acting/modeling career, and of course, you will never have all those kids you said you wanted, Em. Fine. I'll be sure and tell MY kids all about you and how you were a pretty decent person who just had no backbone when it really mattered.

Bud

● ●

Date: April 2, 2005 **Time:** 11:55 p.m. CST.
To: JaniceJin@surftwn.comp
From: Elockhardt@wryword.comp
Subject: *Re: Hang on, EM!*

I ***an***o**t

● ●

Date: April 4, 2005 **Time:** 6:30 pm
To: JoelJin@surftwn.comp
From: Elockhardt@wryword.comp
Subject: *Miss you!*

Hey, JJ! ;-) Hope your plane ride back to CA wasn't too bumpy. We've had enough bumps to deal with lately, haven't we?

Oh Joel, do you remember much of the past few days? After I'd dragged you and Peter to the edge of the book and Bud and Janice pulled us out, it's all kinda become a big blur. I keep asking Bud stuff like, "What did we tell our folks and the police about where we were?" And Bud shakes his head and tells me (for the twelfth or something time), "we told them we were all fed up with school and stuff, and we'd planned to sneak away when Joel came and hide in the woods and have an adventure together. We also told them that you masterminded the whole thing so you could write a book about it."

Huh? A *book about bugs coming out of a book*? Nobody'd ever believe it. That *dufus*.

Anyway, I guess Bud's fort that he'd built last summer helped our case. They knew we had shelter, and Bud had even left a sleeping bag and a bag of saltines there, so it didn't look completely unbelievable, I guess. Peter told his folks the same thing—that he was part of our adventure. He was like a deer in the headlights, Joel, at first wasn't he? I think that he was in shock—so much so, I don't know how much of everything he remembers. He came over yesterday for a visit. He looks older and more confident now. I guess surviving the unsurvivable will do that for you. He's pretty cute now that he's lost so much weight.

Now that I think about it, I guess I'll have plenty of time to write that book ;-) over the five months that Bud and I are grounded.

Oh Joel, so what? I mean it. I am still so grateful that we're all alive; being grounded is practically meaningless to me. I really believe you were close to death...so very close to death.

Thank God, Bud had the great idea to get rid of the book in the incinerator at Dad's sanitation business. Talk about the fire of all fires. I know it's gone for sure now. It has to be. I can't even describe how I feel. I guess it would be free. I feel free. Ironic, since I'm grounded, huh? ;-)

Our lives have been drastically changed over the course of a couple of days. It's just unbelievable. We all sure connected with each other, didn't we? Especially Peter and Janice. She sure got red after he'd hugged her—I'd forgotten she'd had a crush on him in third grade. She must have known he'd turn out to be a hottie. ;-)

I miss you. When are you coming back to Minnesota? I was thinking we're due for a real adventure. (Not funny, eh?)

Em

• •

Date: April 4, 2005 **Time:** 9:30 p.m. CST.
To: KevKaboon@yappers.comp
From: DougKaboon@yappers.comp
Subject: *Bugs, bugs and more bugs (lots of gross ones, too ;-)*

Hey Kevbo, I found the coolest book when I was getting set to load the incinerator. It was just sitting there, halfway out the incinerator door (wonder how it got there?).

Anyway, it looks like one heck of a great read. Get this. It's about bugs—your favorite topic—entolmolgical (or whatever) stuff.

I'll bring it home for you tonight. Kev, this thing has the most realistic pictures I've ever seen. Heh—it almost looks like some of these centipedes' legs are moving…Yeah, sure.

Get to bed before 12—and do your homework for once. Good night, son.

Dad

• •

Date: April 5, 2005 **Time:** 6:30 p.m. CST.
From: MRobins@mned.comp
To: Elockhardt@wryword.comp
Subject: *Re: HELP! To my gorgeous eighth-grade teacher! From her adoring student, Emily Lockhardt*

Dear Emily: My you've certainly surprised us with your antics of late. Although I am disappointed in your conduct I trust that your parents will take the correct steps to properly discipline you. I don't know if you thought about this, but living in the woods as you did, you were surrounded by the very topic of your spring report—which, I might add, is several days overdue. When can I expect you to get that bug report on my desk? It's not going to crawl there on its own, now, is it?

Mrs. Robbins

P.S. You'll never believe what I found in our container of oatmeal…

Karen Laven's award-winning poetry, short fiction and humor essays have appeared in publications across America. She was also a newspaper feature writer and photographer for over seven years. Her nonfiction essay is included in The Healing Project, Voices of Lung Cancer book anthology (LaChance Publishing) and her book-length fiction includes a romance parody, The Surrogate Who Cleaned Up, published by DLSIJ Press, and a fictional contribution to The Insomniac Tales, by Chaucer's Women. She recently moved from Minnesota to Kentucky with her "evil" toy poodle, "Poodie." (Her husband, Doug and two sons, Jake and Luke, also made the trek.)

We hope you enjoyed this book. Your comments and thoughts concerning this book or AMI are welcome.

www.aspirationsmediainc.com

If you're a writer or know of one who has a work that they'd love to see in print – then send it our way. We're always looking for great manuscripts that meet our guidelines. Aspirations Media is looking forward to hearing from you and/or any others you may refer to us.

Thank you for purchasing this
Aspirations Media publication.